DR PILGR

In her first job as a fully-qualified doctor Jane Pilgrim is relieved to think that her new boss will be the kindly old Dr Potts. But Dr Potts dies before she arrives at Northingham Hospital, and Dr Richard Graves, his successor, proves to be a very different—and dangerously attractive—proposition.

Books you will enjoy
in our Doctor Nurse series

DR PILGRIM'S PROGRESS

BY
ANNE VINTON

MILLS & BOON LIMITED
London · Sydney · Toronto

First published in Great Britain 1963
by Mills & Boon Limited, 15–16 Brook's Mews,
London W1A 1DR

© Anne Vinton 1963

Australian copyright 1984
Philippine copyright 1984
This edition 1984

ISBN 0 263 74650 X

Set in 10 on 11 pt Linotron Times
03–0484–55,000

Photoset by Rowland Phototypesetting Ltd
Bury St Edmunds, Suffolk
Made and printed in Great Britain by
Richard Clay (The Chaucer Press) Ltd
Bungay, Suffolk

CHAPTER ONE

JANE PILGRIM awoke with a headache and told herself severely that it served her right. She simply could no longer cope with her mother's kind of life, which involved dinner parties, bridge and drinking and inane conversation which went on until the early hours of the morning.

The headache was the result of such existence, termed by Elaine—her mother—as bringing her darling daughter out of herself. Jane had no desire to be brought out of herself. She was finding it increasingly difficult to understand how such chalk, as was her surviving parent, could have such cheese for her only child. All along the course of Jane's twenty-four years they had clashed about everything under the sun; clothes, schools, boy friends, careers. Fortunately her father had lived long enough to add his weight to his daughter's desire to follow in his footsteps and attend medical school. He had been able to oppose his wife in an attitude of gentle mastery which was the only thing Jane had not learned from him. She was grateful that when he died, suddenly and tragically in an air crash, he had been long sighted enough to endow her chosen career to the conclusion of her six years of study.

Now it was all over, or should be, and today she was expecting the fateful call which would inform her of the results of those long weeks of final examinations.

It was almost not to be borne, the suspense. At the time she had thought the paper work well within her scope, and the vivas had not been at all terrifying. The practicals had found everybody all thumbs, so she was not alone there, and the amount of knowledge requested by the examining bodies, compared with all that had been absorbed during six long years, was to be compared with a small sediment at the bottom of a very large jar.

The class had then been dismissed to take its ease during the weeks of waiting. Some of her classmates had wisely gone vacationing to fit themselves for the impact of the trump of their various dooms, which was very wise of them, and some had probably gone home to suffer and to brood, as she was doing, troubled by afterthoughts and remembering the diagnoses or turns of phrase which had proved so elusive in the examination hall.

Of course it had been impossible to brood much with Elaine in the offing. She would appear, diamond bright, and jog one off to somebody's party, or hold one of her own, or want to go to a theatre in town or simply talk, twenty to the dozen and not saying anything of importance.

'It was a mistake to come home,' she now told the pink ceiling of her bedroom. 'I should have accepted Mick's invitation and joined his party to go climbing in the Pyrenees. I don't think I'm much of a mountaineer but the physical exertion would have been a different kind of challenge. I wonder what I was thinking of?'

She knew very well what she had been thinking of when she refused Mick's invitation, though she still didn't like to admit it even to herself. She had refused because Kent Hillary was to be a member of the same expedition. He was Physics Tutor at the teaching hospital and Jane had been on the brink of falling head over heels in love with him when time had been called by the pressure of examinations, and everyone had been too busy even for such pleasures as falling in love.

If it was a pleasure, Jane now thought cynically. What there had been of it was mostly terrifying in retrospect. Kent had coached her privately on many occasions, been a kindly face and a pair of earnest eyes urging her on. Then, one evening, his eyes had said something else, and she had responded and found, when the dawn had come, that she could not see the tutor in the promise of the lover.

But Kent was married; she had been half aware of this all along without the fact being important to her in any way. But now it became so magnified in its import as to be horrifying. If Kent wanted to remain married, what did he wish Jane to become? She didn't seek the answer, and when Kent casually added his invitation to Mick's, and her head began to spin at the very sound of his voice, she decided to go home to Sussex and take herself apart before she should be tempted to hurl her career into an abyss on the tail of an emotional disaster.

Of course it wasn't really love, she told herself dubiously, it was animal attraction. Discussed frankly and unemotionally in biology classes it had seemed a very manageable thing. There was also that old saw about stolen fruit tasting sweetest. Now it was all over and nobody was hurt.

Nobody was anything, she added to this, somewhat bitterly. She wasn't wiser because she hadn't experienced the sadder part. Kent had aroused in her a hunger of which she hadn't previously been aware, and now she was so aware of it that she felt a part of her was starved and shrivelled.

'Either I'm a doctor or I get married and live what is known as a normal life fulfilling my womanly functions,' she told herself severely. 'I can't have it both ways.'

All mankind had diminished into Kent Hillary,

however. She couldn't imagine falling in love with any-one else.

'And I may not have passed my finals!' she half-groaned. 'Now that I think of it I diagnosed that renal failure all wrongly. That was secondary to the coma and not the cause of it. I'll never be a doctor in a thousand years.'

Mrs Budge, the 'daily', tapped and entered with a tray containing coffee, toast and a brown egg hiding under a yellow cosy.

'Miss Jane, you're talking to yourself again!' she reproved. 'You're letting things get on your nerves. Now have your breakfast and relax. It ain't no good going on. Budge always says when he finishes his pools, "Well, that's it, hit or miss, for another week. Nothing we can do about it once I've stuck her down." It's never any good worrying, I says.'

Jane smiled. The idea of Mr Budge disdaining to regret the fortune he had never possessed and herself failing to attain her life's ambition drew an uncomforting parallel. She *was* worrying. Worrying like hell. The Budge philosophy left her cold.

'Thank you,' she said, as brightly as she could. 'I don't suppose mother's up yet?'

'I don't call Madam till eleven, or so,' Mrs Budge said reprovingly. 'Don't you go disturbing her, Miss Jane. I'm going down, now, to do my dining room. You have another sleep. You look awful.'

Jane eased her breakfast tray aside and went across to the dressing table to see how 'awful' she looked. She saw her face, a pale oval, with dark shadows beneath her hazel, gold flecked eyes. Her hair was tumbled at this hour, golden brown and naturally wavy. Sometimes she regretted this because it would only stay put in one unsophisticated style. Her mother's coiffures were often startling and gave her the illusion of changing her personality.

'But I'm stuck with mine,' she grimaced, and scrambled back into bed to tackle her breakfast, more for Mrs Budge's peace of mind than her own appetite.

The telephone shrilled suddenly in the hall below. The extension, in Elaine Pilgrim's room, had not been switched off and Jane heard her mother grumble sleepily.

'Who can that be at this unearthly hour? I *never* answer the 'phone before midday.'

Elaine switched her 'phone off without bothering to lift the receiver, but the din in the hall went on until Mrs Budge answered it. She lumbered upstairs and opened Jane's door aggressively.

'A young man for *you*, Miss Jane,' she said disapprovingly. 'And me in the middle of my dining room.'

Jane passed her at a sprint, her headache disappearing quickly.

'Jane Pilgrim here,' she announced into the mouthpiece.

'Hello, Jane! Dr Cole here. I said *Dr* Cole, speaking.'

'Yes, I heard you, Doctor. Did you wish to speak to Mother?'

She didn't know a Dr Cole and presumed him to be an acquaintance of her late father's.

'Twerp!' the voice shed years in as many seconds. 'Denis Cole, you juggins! I've passed. I've just heard the good tidings.'

'Oh, Denis, I'm so glad. Well done! I knew you'd pass.'

'Well, *I* didn't. I'm mightily relieved. I feel quite ill with relief. What about you?'

'I haven't heard yet. I suppose they let you know just the same if—if you haven't got through?'

'If I've done it, Jane, you're a certainty. Don't fret.'

'Nothing's certain until it's happened, Denis. You're cheering from the other side of the fence at the moment. Have you heard about anybody else?'

'Mark's through, and Olga. You could ring up the hospital, of course, and ask somebody to look at the results for you. They'll be up on the board by now.'

'I should hate to be told I'd failed by a second party. No, I'll wait. Once again, heartiest congratulations, Denis.'

She replaced the receiver and trailed back upstairs. It was almost ten a.m. The telephone shrilled again and she turned in her tracks mumbling, 'Somebody else to congratulate, I suppose.' In a louder voice she called: 'I'll get it, Mrs Budge.'

The voice on the 'phone was brisk and impersonal. 'I have a telegram for Miss Jane Pilgrim. Confirmation will follow in the usual way. Shall I read it to you?'

'Do, please,' she said in a voice which, suddenly, belonged to an automaton. She felt so calm as not to be quite true.

'The message reads: "Miss Jane Pilgrim stop You have been successful in satisfying the examining body of the British Medical Association stop Henceforward you may practise as a doctor stop Congratulations stop."'

'Stop, stop, stop,' went round and round in Jane's brain suddenly. Her calmness was a myth. She was feeling faint and happy and miserable and inadequate at one and the same time.

The impersonal voice was asking if she should repeat the message.

'No—no, thank you. Thank you, very much.'

'Very good, Dr Pilgrim.'

Dr Pilgrim! Jane replaced the receiver and smiled tremulously. So the impersonal voice was attached to a person, after all, who had recognised the import of the news.

She had done it and could call herself Doctor at long last. There would be the ceremony of taking the oath, of course, but the important preliminaries had borne fruit and hers would henceforward be the privilege of serving mankind.

Her father, who had been a consultant surgeon, would have been so proud of her at this moment.

Her mother—well, Elaine was a different kettle of fish and her reactions to the news could not be guessed. She had hated the discipline of her daughter's years of training, was bored by talk of illness and operation, being blessed with good health herself; she was of a hedonistic nature and failed to understand anybody who did the unpleasant jobs of life without having the economical need to do so.

Jane tiptoed next door to her mother's room feeling this was a moment she had to share with someone. Elaine stirred among her pillows, saying, fretfully: 'What ails everyone this morning? The telephone keeps ringing and some wretched bird imagines it's spring. You're all of a fidget, Jane. What is it? If I must be disturbed why haven't you brought my Alka-Seltzer and my coffee?'

Jane sat down on the bed, her excitement spilling over.

'Mother, I heard this morning that I've passed my finals. I'm a doctor. They just 'phoned the telegram through.'

Elaine slowly raised herself on one elbow. She was one of those rare people who still look pretty in bed. She was waxen skinned and her pale hair was tinted lavender and caught up in a beribboned boudoir cap. Her eyes were very blue and shorter sighted than she would ever admit. Now they gazed unwinkingly at her daughter.

'That takes me back,' she sighed. 'I was already married to your father and heard his great news—in bed like this—the day he heard he'd qualified. Why must you look so like your father?' she demanded. 'Sometimes I think you are no part of me at all.'

'Mummy, I can't help what I look like and every child has two parents to start with.'

Elaine was still investigating the past, however.

'From that day on I began to play second fiddle. I hated it, of course, but I had to lump it because I loved him. It's the devil loving a man more than he loves you. See that you don't make the same mistake, my girl. Yes, I heard that he'd qualified and then I watched him grow in professional stature. From MD to Fellow and then into surgery to his Master's certificate. And all the time he was growing away from me, his wife, and oh! so subtly.'

'Mother,' Jane almost pleaded. 'Daddy always loved you. He did.'

'Did he?' Elaine asked sharply. 'I wonder. I don't suppose I was always very lovable. However, what was it you were saying, dear?'

'I came to tell you that I'd passed my finals, Mother. Aren't you going to wish me luck—all that sort of thing?'

'I wish you luck, Jane, but even more I wish you happiness. You'll find in a doctor's profession that a successful career and happiness are not always synonymous. Other's people's problems become your problems; other people's lives become your life until your own identity becomes a complex of other identities. Doctors should marry other doctors. Being a wife-in-waiting can be lonely and frustrating. Anyway, I wish you all you want of it, Jane. Now I shall lose you, too, if I haven't lost you already. But not to worry. I have hosts of friends.'

Jane felt she understood her mother much better for this conversation. Perhaps Elaine had been lonely and frustrated and resentful; perhaps her father's success had meant only the thin veneer of a happy home life. Perhaps this was why the house was now always filled with people who made her mother feel important and self-assured.

But Jane could not feel sad that her own ambitions were being encouraged by success. The party atmosphere might suit Elaine very nicely, but her daughter was made of sterner stuff and would probably never find her life's happiness until she had climbed the hill of difficulty which—no doubt—lay somewhere ahead of the young Dr Pilgrim.

CHAPTER TWO

WHEN Jane returned after the recess to St Christopher's, the famous teaching hospital where she had qualified, she was immediately involved in a series of celebrations for the successful candidates. She and Olga Wyatt joined forces and gave one on their own behalf, and the unsuccessful students were gradually cheered and spurred on to make a further assault by the warming effects of alcohol and their comrades' assurances that they would be sure to pull it off 'next time'.

It was on one of these occasions that Jane found herself sipping champagne while sharing a sofa arm with Kent Hillary in the students' common room. She had received his official congratulations, as she had from her other tutors, but suddenly she felt as though she was alone with him, his eyes fastened on hers so that she could see the green lights in them and his voice low and intimate.

'Why didn't you come with us?' he asked her.

'You mean—climbing?' she countered, her heart doing peculiar things in her chest. 'I'm no mountaineer.'

'Half the party wasn't. But there were—distractions. I wouldn't have gone myself only Mick said he'd asked *you*.'

'I—I went home,' Jane stated, feeling light headed like someone who has breathed too much oxygen. 'I couldn't have settled to anything until the results came through.'

'What will you be doing now?'

'A job you mean? Oh, I don't really know. I may go

north. I would like to work in a nice little provincial hospital, doing bits of everything.'

'I could, you know, put in a word for you to stay on here as one of Voegel's housemen.'

'Could you?'

Dr Voegel was the consultant who was attached both to the hospital and the medical school. He was an Austrian and well known in the field of medicine. It was accounted a signal honour to become attached to such an eminent personage so early in one's career.

'Then we could continue to see a bit of one another,' Kent went on, meaningly.

'Please get me another drink,' Jane said quickly, adding: 'I'd like to think about it, naturally, Kent.'

While he was away joining the scramble for food and drink Jane was joined by Olga, who had been her friend throughout medical school days.

'You have the fixed look of a small bird about to be devoured by a snake,' she said bluntly. 'What dreamy nothings has he been whispering into your shell-like eustachian tubes?'

'You mean Kent?'

'Of course I mean Kent. The Casanova of St Christopher's. Who else?'

'Actually we were discussing jobs. Kent said he may be able to put in a word for me with Dr Voegel.'

'And why should he do that, I wonder?'

'Possibly he thinks I'd do rather well on a medical firm.'

'And just possibly his thoughts may not be quite so pure. Remember that, my dear. You do know, of course, that Mrs Hillary is suing for divorce? It's in the undefended list. This morning's paper, in case you haven't got around to reading it. I see the handsome devil returning so I'll buzz off and hope you have enough sense to heed the gipsy's warning.'

Jane's face was like a peony as Kent handed her a second glass of champagne. Was he allowing his wife to divorce him with a view to—?

She curbed this trend of thought and came to a quick decision.

'Kent—thank you for offering to put a word in for me with Dr Voegel. It's very kind of you, but I really would like to make my own way in my career. I think that if one starts—like that—one may always feel dubious about one's own abilities. You do understand?'

'My dear Jane, you'll find you need all sorts of a leg up in this lark. There aren't enough jobs for the boys, let alone a dainty little filly like you. I should know—'

'Well, good luck!' he said somewhat sulkily, a moment later, in the sort of voice which means just the opposite. Shortly after that he drifted away to chat with Penny Jemingway, an attractive fourth year student with flaming red hair.

Jane was left feeling unaccountably depressed and was relieved when she could drift back to the room she rented in a small street close to the hospital.

Supposing she had difficulty getting fixed up with a job and had turned Kent's offer down only to live to know the bitterness of regret? Because two people found they were physically attractive to one another, was it to be considered a sin and a shame?

That was an old fashioned foible and she was running away from something which had never really started.

All this she argued and more while she sat brushing her hair in front of the mottled dressing table mirror and saw her own face, as though for the first time, looking troubled and pale in the poor light her landlady considered adequate.

'What you're afraid of, Jane, is accepting something

for which there's the possibility you may be required to pay later in a different coin. As a doctor you have a responsibility to your job. There should be no other strings attached to it. That's why you turned Kent down and probably offended him for life. So where do we go from here?'

A few days later she knew the answer to that, when— with several letters out to various hospital boards—she received an invitation to call for an interview at Northingham Royal Infirmary. She looked Northingham up on the map. It was a small country town between Carlisle and Newcastle-upon-Tyne with a population of fifty-odd thousand souls. It sounded like the sort of place where one might well gain a very general experience.

Of course it was a long way from home, but that was all in its favour seeing that she wouldn't be required to visit Elaine very often.

Jane was aware of the pricking of her conscience the moment she had aired such an uncharitable thought.

If only Elaine didn't have such impossible friends, she immediately defended herself; friends such as Harry Esher, with his loud voice and saloon bar personality.

'Still, I'll go and see Mother when I've been up to Northingham,' she told herself. 'I may have some definite news about my future by then.'

The new young doctors were by now disappearing to various parts of the country on the same mission as that on which she was soon to be bound. Mick Lewis went off to Lancashire; Olga considered herself lucky to gain employment in a London hospital, for competition for these posts was always great. She was making a start under the wing of an eminent pathologist. She had failed twice in her pathology exam so was obviously going to know a great deal more about her weak subject before very long. Mark Phelps was bound for an interview in

Jersey, and Denis Cole, along with two others, was being considered for the vacancy on Dr Voegel's 'firm'.

Jane went off from King's Cross, one bleak winter morning, without having seen Kent Hillary to say good-bye. He was apparently sulking a little with her and she felt vaguely unsettled whenever she thought of him. The further north she travelled, however, the more she appeared to be entering another dimension. It was not so much distance as accepting the irrevocable fact that St Christopher's was now behind her with all its ac-complishments, problems, memories and friends. Whether or not she landed the job in Northingham she would still have to get a job somewhere. The training hospital considered her to be off its hands. She was henceforward on her own.

'The Forest of Sherwood', she read from the train. Was there really a forest of that name? she pondered. Had Robin Hood, then, existed outside of someone's lively imagination? The forest was black and bleak on a day such as this, for most of the trees were deciduous and reached bare, cold arms to the leaden sky. The whole country of Yorkshire lay under a mantle of snow, which was still falling, and although much rolling stock lay apparently forgotten in blocked sidings, the mighty express continued to roar its way northwards without let or hindrance.

This was a part of Britain she had never visited in her life before, which she now considered most neglectful. She knew the continent intimately, yet had only once motored to Scotland with her parents. Then they had gone up the other side, on the A6, and the weather had been so miserable that it had coloured all her impres-sions and lessened her desire to repeat the performance.

It was warm in the train, however, and she gained an

impression of wide open country with rolling moors, rich areas of agricultural land and grey, dour little towns and villages with a stalwart individuality all their own.

She detrained at Newcastle-upon-Tyne and where she had been expecting a depressed slum area found a wide, handsome town with shops and streets reminiscent of London at its best and with everything much more conveniently to hand. Everyone was so friendly, too, so that it was like coming home.

A porter, who had adopted her as a 'foreigner' and advised her of the best place to lunch away from the atmosphere of trains and stations, now took her under his wing again and shepherded her on to a local train which would deposit her in Northingham.

'Take you as long to get there as you've come, hinny,' he told her. 'She's slow is the two-thirty. Pity you haven't a car. Be there in less than an hour. Remember the hospital is straight up the hill facing the station. I used to be on the signals at Northingham before my eyesight failed a bit.'

She tried to tip the kindly man but he would have none of it.

'Normally I take all I can get from Londoners,' he twinkled at her. Jane was to discover that 'Londoners' included everybody minus a northern accent. 'But not from you, hinny. It wouldn't be friendly.'

Hereabouts there was no snow lying but the promise of it was in the bitter wind driving low cloud across Hadrian's Wall. The train was slow and fussy and apparently gave right of way to every freight train on the track as it was always hooting itself to a stop and waiting miles from anywhere until something in more of a hurry thundered by. It was after four before they steamed into Northingham and the daylight had disappeared in an unpleasant, driving sleet.

Jane's feet were frozen and she wished she had worn fur-lined boots. She had dressed sensibly, as she thought; but whereas a medium heeled court shoe was adequate at all times for London pavements, with taxis always at one's beck, here it was different for the sleet made the pavements slippery and the one and only taxi which served the station had been whisked away by a tired businessman anxious to get home to his fireside and his tea.

She plodded up the hill opposite the station as directed, not thinking very highly of Northingham or its amenities. Originally she had wanted to work in a small town, not thinking that towns are usually small because of their inaccessibility or lack of social facilities. When she saw what was obviously a hospital facing her, however, with its windows bright in the general gloom, she cheered up perceptibly. She supposed that if there was a hospital in Timbuctoo it would have a similar effect on one. A hospital was one's field of operation. A blacksmith must feel the same way whenever he sniffed hot steel or saw a pair of bellows.

She made herself known at a desk marked *Inquiries* in the Outpatients' Hall, deserted at this hour, and sat down to wait on a hard bench while she wriggled her numbed toes. Here it was quiet but there was a muted din in the background suggestive of the life with which she had grown familiar. There was the rattle of teacups and the rush of busy, rubber soled feet, the whine of a lift and the sound of wheels, trolley wheels, chair wheels, ambulance wheels.

A couple of white coats flashed past her vision and she heard a snatch of conversation.

'She's the little blonde in Casualty. You ought to watch out. That limpid look is the result of years of practice.'

'Men!' thought Jane, 'and their one-track minds.'

She also pondered that the two housemen were already doing the jobs for which they had been trained. She still had to impress somebody sufficiently to win that very right for herself.

'Dr Pilgrim?' inquired a tall, dark girl. She held a sheaf of cardboard covers in her arms and was obviously a secretary of sorts. 'I think Dr Potts wants to see you. He's doing an examination at the moment but he asked me to see that you get tea. Will you come with me, please?'

'Thank you,' Jane murmured, wondering if Dr Potts was young, old, nice or harsh with his juniors.

She followed Miss Pryce, as the young woman introduced herself, into a cheerful room where, in addition to the central heating, a gas fire had also been lit. There was a typewriter at a table in front of the window, where Miss Pryce immediately ensconsed herself.

'I'll get on if you don't mind, Doctor,' she indicated the file covers. 'Dr Potts does make such lengthy notes on every patient. It'll take the best part of a week to do this lot and I have Mr France's to do, too. Your tea will be along. I ordered it on my way down.'

The typewriter began to tap out its merry rhythm and a sepia-eyed Barbadian maid entered the room with a tray which she set down at Jane's elbow.

'I can never spell "Sclerosis",' complained Miss Pryce. 'Is there an "h" in it or not, Doctor?'

'Not,' smiled Jane.

The tea was warming and she was feeling very much happier. She had never even spoken to a member of the clerical staff at Christopher's. They had appeared to be a race apart.

Suddenly she wanted to start work there and then; to read the case histories for herself and discover who was suffering from 'Sclerosis'; what form it took.

'Miss Pryce,' she ventured, 'is it all right if I talk to you? Will it distract you to answer a few questions?'

CHAPTER THREE

'ACTUALLY,' the girl smiled, 'I had better stop and sort out my notes. Ask away, Doctor. What is it you wish to know?'

'Well,' Jane cleared her throat, 'I'm newly qualified as you have probably guessed. I came in answer to the hospital advertisement. I haven't heard of Dr Potts before. I presume he requires a houseman?'

'There are two vacancies, actually,' the secretary explained. 'One medical and one surgical. It doesn't really matter where you start because you change with the other one after six months.'

Jane realised that 'you' was not meant personally in this case.

'Mr France went home at four o'clock, however, after seeing the other four. Dr Potts stayed on to see you and then this emergency was admitted.'

'So there are five of us?' Jane inquired, thinking it augured ill that the surgeon had gone home without seeing her. He must have been well enough satisfied with the other candidates.

'Yes. There were six, but one doctor, from Edinburgh, whom Dr Potts fancied, was taken ill with shingles. They say nerves can bring that on.'

'Nerves are accountable for much,' Jane agreed. 'Mine don't feel so good at the moment.'

Miss Pryce laughed.

'Don't lose heart, Doctor. While there's life there's hope.'

There was a boom like a cannon in the corridor and

the secretary announced: 'That sounds like Doctor now.'

'Well!' Dr Potts was large, shaggy, genial and happy. 'So you've arrived, love.' His accent was broad Yorkshire. 'Well, George, how d'you think she'll do, eh?' He turned to the resident physician who looked as though he was trying to say the right thing but didn't know quite what that was in the circumstances. 'Five foot four: sit down, love; take your weight off your feet: looks willing and is as pretty as a picture. What do you think, George? We've never had a lass. Let's give her a try.'

Jane drew breath rather noisily, thus saving 'George' from expressing an opinion.

'Don't you want to know what I can do, sir?' she piped, not recognising the voice as her own.

'Not particularly, love,' boomed Dr Potts. 'I know you must be qualified or you wouldn't be here, but that doesn't mean much to me. It's now you begin to learn, with real people choking on their own phlegm, like one poor devil I've just seen, not somebody trying to raise a cough for your benefit at medical school. Some you'll kill and some you'll cure. I naturally like the balance to be the right way round. But if you're willing and honest and keep your pretty head down to the right size, then I'll stand right behind you when some fool sues you for your skin because somebody left things too late and you failed to raise a Lazarus. Added to all that you'll cheer up these old eyes when they're tired and jaded at the end of a long day. Yes, George, I think we'll take this lass. She's bonny. What's your name again, love?'

'Pilgrim, sir. Jane Pilgrim.'

'A grand name. It's my favourite hymn, you know. "To be a pilgrim",' he bellowed in a great *basso profundo* of a voice, ignoring Miss Pryce's obvious hysterics at the performance. 'Right. Come on, George. I want to get home to my tea. Goodnight, love!'

'Er—excuse me, sir,' Jane said hastily. 'Am I to understand the job is mine?'

'Bar the shouting, love. Bar the shouting. The Hospital Board meets tomorrow, as you'll have been told. They like to think they're doing the appointing, but *we* get in first and make up our own minds. After all, anything might come out of an egg, even a cuckoo. If they give us a cuckoo we simply pluck him and drive him away, so we still get who we wanted in the end. They'll see to you, love. Mrs Potts will be raving.'

'Goodnight, sir, and—and thank you for waiting to see me.'

'It has been a pleasure, love. Now, George—' The boom died away down the corridor without George having said a single word.

Jane sank back limply into her chair.

'I—I don't know what to think,' she said weakly. 'He's rather overpowering, isn't he?'

'A great character,' smiled Miss Pryce. 'He's exactly like that on the wards. The patients all love him and he has the effect of a tonic on them. I don't mind how much work I do for Dr Potts, but'—she smiled ruefully—'I can see I had better do an hour's overtime this evening. It's half past five, now.'

'And I'm distracting you,' Jane said uncertainly. 'What do I do now, I wonder?'

'The others are being accommodated in the town overnight,' the secretary confided. 'But because you were travelling such a long way they're putting you up in the hospital. I'll ring for a maid and she'll take you to your room. The doctors have supper at eight o'clock.'

Still feeling as though a steam roller had run over her, Jane found herself in a spartan little bed-sitting room with somebody else's books on the shelves, obviously someone interested in surgery to judge by the titles. The text books were interspersed with some rather lurid paper-backs of the whodunnit variety and Jane tried to read to pass an hour away. But it was so long since she had really been able to lose herself in fiction that she gave up the attempt and began to collect her thoughts.

Dr Potts had said the job was hers, but could she really be sure? Obviously Mr France, the consultant surgeon, also had some weight to carry in the selection of the candidates, seeing that the chosen one would automatically be moving on to him after six months.

Jane was really attracted to the physical side of medicine, and had no desire to specialise in surgery, but as a junior she needed her full quota of experience in all fields. If one day she should decide to be a general practitioner there was much minor surgery one was required to do there and then on the spot. If she ever wanted a change and applied for a job as ship's doctor she would be required to perform appendicectomies, and the like, perhaps in difficult circumstances, without fainting all over the ship's hospital floor.

But she knew where her true leanings lay, and Mr France might spot this at the interview and advise for the appointment of somebody else.

Suddenly Jane loved this little hospital and wanted to work here more than any other place on earth. Nobody could be quite like Dr Potts. He must be the Father Christmas of all consultants, as big-hearted as he was big-bodied. After only a few minutes she felt that she could soon love him; that he would automatically take over that secret place in her heart which had remained locked since her father's sudden death.

A tap came on the door and without getting up off the bed, where she was sprawling full length, she called

'Come in!' expecting it to be one of the maids informing her of the whereabouts of the doctors' dining room.

It was a man who entered, however; a creature of such aquiline good looks and arrogance he might have been a Roman centurion.

'Good evening,' he addressed her in a clear, incisive unaccented voice. 'I am obviously *not* addressing Dr Waddell.'

Jane, who had kicked off her shoes, shot upright in a confusion of embarrassment and now succeeded in getting her right foot encased but not the left. She wobbled a little and said: 'I—er—don't know who—er—who lives here usually, sir.'

Why she should address him as 'sir' she couldn't imagine. He might be a visitor for one of the patients for all she knew. There are some people, however, who wear an air to which one automatically defers. He was one of these, though he couldn't be more than thirty-eight at the very most.

'I can tell you Dr Waddell does normally live here, Miss, Madam, whoever you are,' the arrogant one proceeded. 'Possibly he has retired to the sick bay with a bout of food poisoning. Yesterday's fish was decidedly off. Is somebody hiding you in here?'

It was some moments before his implication sank in and indignation rose in her breast like gall.

'Certainly not!' she said, her face like a peony. 'I have done nothing to merit being hidden anywhere. I am here for the night with the hospital's full knowledge and consent.' Having succeeded in donning both shoes she drew herself to her full height and took the initiative. 'Can I help you?' she asked politely.

'Possibly not, thank you,' he declined, with an acid little smile. 'You can act as witness, however. I am taking back the book the said Dr Waddell has failed to return.' He took down one of the mightier tomes from the bookshelf. 'Sorry to have disturbed your siesta,' he smiled again, and withdrew from the room.

Just as Jane had been drawn by the warmth of Dr Potts she was repelled by this stranger. He was like an electric fence, she pondered, and about as comfortable. How dared he suggest that she was keeping an assignation by occupying this room while its owner was away? No doubt such things occasionally went on, but they didn't happen when she was one of the parties concerned. She felt affronted and slandered by the suggestion and nursed her injury until supper time, when she felt no better at finding the stranger sharing the same long table but at the far end, while she was with the lesser fry.

The two young doctors who had passed the remark about the blonde nurse in Casualty tried to engage her in conversation, but she did not yet feel herself to be one of them and also she didn't wish them to discuss *her* behind her back. At least she would give them no cause to, anyhow. Her gaze returned to the handsome man. Did he also work here? He was obviously on familiar terms with the senior members of the staff. She tried to catch his name. It sounded like 'Gray' but she later found out that it was Graves.

Before the meal ended there was a commotion of 'bleeps' from every doctor's pocket. They all disappeared like one man, grumbling, and Jane was left self-consciously regarding Richard Graves quietly eating an apple at the other end of the table.

'I should get your coffee,' he advised, without looking at her. 'No doubt if there is some emergency someone will inform us sooner or later.'

There was an emergency, and one of the younger housemen came and advised Richard Graves of it a few minutes later.

'It appears,' he again addressed a spot above Jane's head, 'that a thirty-two seater bus filled with happy revellers has skidded on an icy patch and gone over the bank into a ravine a few miles out of the town. That means thirty-three customers if they are all surviving, which I shouldn't think very likely. I intend to go and do what I can. If you have nothing better to do would you care to come along?'

Jane forgot to be offended in the honour of being asked to serve as a member of her profession. She rushed to grab her coat and tagged on with Richard Graves who had acquired a very businesslike black bag. He found time to regard her shoes.

'I presume you have nothing else with you?'

'No—er—I haven't.'

'Scrambling down the ravine you would probably get a fracture and be no use to anyone. What size?'

'Four,' she said rather shortly.

The next moment, it seemed, she was equipped with more suitable gum-boots and was scrambling into the heated interior of a large car beside the man she had decided she loathed.

'In one day I've met both the nicest and nastiest of men,' she pondered, and then she held on to her seat as the big car went at great speed through narrow lanes to the scene of the accident.

Police were on the spot and had cordoned off the area. They had erected spotlights and helpers were already down crawling like ants round the wrecked coach which had trapped its occupants inside.

'They'll be haemorrhaging to death,' decided Richard Graves, viewing the splintered glass with a trained eye. 'And the damned thing's wrong way up. I wish the fire people would get here and end one hazard.'

'Oh, dear! oh, dear!' Jane fluttered.

'This is no time for asking what can the matter be!' he said irritably. 'If I can put you inside can you reconnoitre and fix a few tourniquets?'

'I'll try,' she said.

'Good! Here comes the Fire Brigade, anyhow. I shall worry less about you on that account. I would go in myself, if I could, but I'm about twice your size.'

'That's all right, sir.'

He picked her up bodily and eased her through one of the bus windows, which he had knocked clear of glass.

'Here's a torch,' he told her, and she made the most uncomfortable journey of her young life, bent almost double and hampered by inert, injured bodies.

As fast as she made examination and applied tourniquets, Richard Graves shoved further supplies in to her. Where the injured were conscious and in pain she gave injections of morphia, carefully labelling each recipient. All the while a man wearing a mask was working with an oxyacetylene welder cutting a hole in the side of the bus, the emergency exit having jammed, and the fire hoses played foam on the escaping petrol.

It seemed ages before other willing hands joined hers and she was able to crawl out and stretch her aching back and limbs.

'Well done!' Richard Graves congratulated her quietly.

Criticism she could have tolerated at that juncture, but not kindness. She was so weary and affected by the personal side of the accident that she suddenly crumpled up and wept.

'It was horrible!' she moaned as she found herself drawn close to a strong chest for a moment, a large white handkerchief thrust into her hands.

'It always is,' he said kindly. 'But one gets used to such things in time. You've been well and truly blooded and there can never be a first time for you again. Have a good blow and come and help me fasten some splints. They're coming out in goodly numbers now and need to be despatched as quickly as possible.'

Once more Jane was drawn into the never-ending battle to save human life.

After the tiredness was past she felt peculiarly exalted and wouldn't have changed places with anyone.

CHAPTER FOUR

'HE sounds a real poppet,' opined Olga, when the two friends met a few days later in London. She had been hearing all about Dr Potts, Consultant Physician to the Northingham and District Hospital Management Committee, and was imagining a person who was a cross between James Robertson Justice and Santa Claus.

'Oh, he is,' Jane said with emphasis. 'He's such a natural person, too. If he was attending the Queen he would call Her Majesty "love" and probably tell her to take the weight off her feet.'

They both laughed.

'My chief is so affected,' complained Olga, 'I shall probably never know what he's really like. He calls me "Miss", as though he disapproves of women doctors.'

'So many of them still do,' Jane nodded. She hadn't mentioned Richard Graves to Olga and wondered at her own reticence on this subject. Goodness knows she had been through enough with him, what with one thing and another, and even exposed her weakness to him in tears, the form shock had taken with her.

'And how did the interview with the Board go?' Olga wanted to know.

'Oh, quite well, I suppose. Dr Potts was rather naughty, and answered all the questions they asked me before I had a chance to open my mouth. For instance, when the Chairman asked me what subject in the curriculum I was most conversant with, Dr Potts chipped in with, "What the heck does that matter? I'd be happier if she was conversant with none of 'em and knew a bit about 'em all." Then Mr France, the surgeon, asked me the procedure for an emergency Caesarean section. That's about the one thing I did know so I thanked my lucky stars. After that the Chairman referred to a letter which someone had sent'—again she avoided referring to Richard Graves, though she knew the sender must have been he—'commending me on my initiative, courage and obedience in the face of an emergency. It was really quite embarrassing because at the time I was terrified and I'm sure I could never go through all that again.'

'You have all the luck,' Olga said enviously, having heard of the accident. 'If I had been there I could have done all the blood-groupings on the spot and earned myself a pat on the back.'

'You think of all you might have done,' Jane said with a shudder of remembrance. 'But at the time you feel sick and your hands are slippery with blood. You don't think about the group, only how to stop it, and then you find you're working on a dead man and he becomes horrifyingly unimportant. You have to get on with the living.'

Olga's hand rested sympathetically on her friend's for an instant.

'It has made you grow up, Jane,' she said wisely. 'Some people do it slowly. You've accomplished it at a bound. I suppose you still don't know whether you've got the job or not?'

'No.' Jane grimaced. 'They told me they would let me know, though Dr Potts gave me an outsize wink and the thumbs up sign as I left the room. One has to be patient.'

She spent a couple of days winding things up at her London lodgings where a new medical student was waiting to take over. She managed to dispose of many of her books to the new tenant and was also in the happy position of being able to give advice from the eminence of her new status as a doctor.

'Watch Dr Watts. He's inclined to skip over details as being unimportant, but in the exams the details gain more attention than the facts. You have to keep pressing him to enlarge. Don't forget that. Then there's Sir Wilfrid; he likes to think all students are congenital idiots. It's best to allow him this because he takes you through his subject slowly and thoroughly and if anybody's too bright, or impertinent, he sulks, and then nobody gets anywhere.'

There was nothing to keep her in London any longer, and so Jane went to Hawk's Mead and her mother.

The Surrey landscape was gripped in the iron hand of frost but the house was centrally heated and warm. This did not mean that it was comfortable, however, for Elaine was impossible to approach on the subject of her daughter's career.

'And where is Northingham?' she asked coldly.

Jane described its geographical position as well as she was able.

'Oh, gracious! These depressed areas usually foster horrible epidemics of one sort or another.'

'Mother, it is *not* a depressed area. It is a very nice little country town with enormous civic pride. Even if it was—as you put it—a depressed area, I could not, as a doctor, afford to turn my nose up at it. You have the Home Counties' mind which imagines all provincials still wear woad.'

'Jane, don't be rude.'

'I'm sorry, Mother. I have no right to criticise. I was inclined to think as you do before I saw for myself how much there is of England north of the Thames.'

'They have the most horrible accents, though. Deny that if you can.'

'I find the various accents charming, the people genuine.'

'Meaning I'm not?'

'Did I say that?' Jane was rapidly growing exasperated. 'Mother, we always seem to be quarrelling.'

'Well, it's not my fault. If your only daughter came to tell you that she was going hundreds of miles away to a job she could well have done in the next town, you might feel inclined to be quarrelsome also.'

'I haven't got the job yet. In any case we have to get ourselves fixed up where we can during this first year. Later on, if I go into a practice, I may find one nearer home.'

'Here comes Harry,' Elaine announced gladly as a tweed-suited rather pompous figure came up the drive. 'Dear old Harry. He comes to see me every single day.'

Jane had her suspicions that Harry Esher was courting her mother. The idea of Harry with his balding pate, loose wet mouth and paunch usurping her father's place nauseated Jane not a little.

'Would you like me to go out for a walk?' she inquired.

'Darling, how delicate of you!' Elaine laughed, smoothing her lavender hair and making her daughter suddenly aware that she was only forty-five years old. 'No, stay and talk to Harry. He's been awfully depressed for a week, poor darling! It's nerves, or something. He's usually such good fun, as you know.'

Harry was admitted and came and stood immediately with his back to the log fire.

'As though he's already master of the house,' Jane thought darkly.

Elaine laughed at all five of Harry's opening gambits, and then the visitor addressed himself to the daughter.

He was a Queen's Counsel by profession but always appeared to be able to afford long periods when he did nothing at all.

'Dr Pilgrim, MD, I believe?' he now said heartily.

'Not yet,' Jane was able to correct him. 'I have to work for my MD. That's another exam altogether.'

'Oh, my poor dear. It must be exactly like the Law which demands that one must be tottering on the edge of the grave before one is anybody at all.'

'Oh, come, Harry. Surely *you're* somebody and *you're* not dead yet?'

'Thank you, my dear, but I'm only poorly. My own doctor says I'll be a new man if I lose some weight. Supposing I ask for a second opinion. Yours?'

Elaine laughed delightedly, but Jane heard a chord of remembrance crashing in her brain. It had been the morning of her interview with the Northingham Hospital Board and she had been prowling around trying to look at everything without getting in anybody's way. Then, in the doorway of the Medical Ward, she had seen Dr Potts and the inarticulate 'George'.

'Listen, lad, I'm not interested in what the tests show. The best test *I* know, and you'll ever know, is how a patient says he feels. It's no good a million tests proving he's all right if he says he's all wrong. Nobody wants to feel poorly. It's a ruddy bore. When your tests and your patient agree, then he's all right. But always believe your patient where there's a doubt.'

Harry was joking about himself for Elaine's benefit, but Jane was now seeing him as a doctor, and there was a greyish texture to his usually ruddy countenance. He was overweight, of course, but there was something more than that. When he knocked a lamp over it took three attempts before he grasped and righted it again. There were beads of sweat on his forehead and his right hand trembled slightly so that he shoved it into his pocket to still it.

'Beastly nerves,' he complained. 'I must keep off the old alcohol for a bit.'

'Mother,' Jane said that evening, 'you're not thinking of marrying again, are you?'

'Why not? I mean chance would be a fine thing, but would you have any objection?'

'I think I would, frankly. I should hate you to marry Harry.'

'Why Harry? He has position and he amuses me.'

'He's so much older than you are.'

'Rubbish! He's fifty and brilliant in his job.'

'Well, he seems to be ageing much faster than you are. I thought he looked quite old today.'

'He's a bit off colour, that's all. If I want to marry Harry I won't ask your consent, darling daughter. You go off into the wilds and leave me to make my own bed.'

'I hope it's of roses, Mother. I really do.'

'Bless you!' said Elaine, smiling. 'That's a very sweet thing to say. But who wants to lie on roses? Think of all those thorns . . . !'

A couple of days later Jane heard officially that she had been selected to serve as medical house-assistant at Northingham Royal Infirmary.

Temporarily her cup of joy and thankfulness ran quite over.

Days of absolute wonderment followed for Jane, despite the bitterness of the winter weather which had brought deep, frozen snow even to southern areas. She felt justified in indulging in a spending spree, not only buying things she needed for her new job but also other trivia which she had denied herself previously because she had felt unable to afford them from her modest allowance.

Now she took pleasure in having her new, white, doctor's coats tailored to her slight figure, and she bought a brand-new stethoscope with ivory earpieces and both an ophthalmoscope and auriscope. The black bag, which was the symbol of her new profession, was now looking quite businesslike whenever she opened it to view the contents.

She also bought some new clothes; a warmly lined camel hair coat, a pair of laced walking shoes (she imagined Richard Graves would approve of them if she ever met him again) and a couple of cocktail dresses in case Northingham Infirmary was ever inclined for the gaiety of social occasions.

She sent her luggage on ahead and made a quick round of her friends, during her last week, staying a night with Olga, who was called out in the small hours on some pathological emergency and so was not present in the morning to wish her friend God speed; a couple of days with a married friend from her school days and the rest of the time with her godmother, who was always delighted to see her.

'I'm so proud of you, darling,' said Mrs Ingerton, a charming widow who was, herself, childless. 'But I always said you'd make it, didn't I? Now that you're a doctor, and everything, I wonder if I could solicit your advice?'

'Professionally?' Jane laughed. 'You naughty thing! You know that would be most unethical. What's the trouble?'

'Well, it's not sufficient to bother my own doctor with, I feel sure. I see double on occasions. It goes all right after a few minutes but it's disconcerting while it lasts. I usually get a background headache when it happens.'

Suddenly Jane wanted to turn round and run away. She didn't want to be a doctor at all; didn't want to know what was wrong with this woman who had always been so kind and understanding with her.

It might be nothing or it might be everything and it seemed peculiarly unfair that one should have to worry about people close and dear to one. Patients were always other people, not one's own loved and dear ones.

'We'll go and see Dr Wilkinson tomorrow, shall we, dear?' she heard herself advise. 'It could mean one of fifty different things. I'm not experienced in diagnoses yet, Aunt Irene. Give me time. But I do think whatever is wrong ought to be tackled in the early stages. The doctor's general lament is "If only people would come to us in time!" So I'm not going to pretend to guess what's wrong with you. I'm going to be a good doctor and make you do the proper thing. Now lead me to a cup of tea and some of your madeira cake. Nobody makes it quite like you do and I need the calories now that I'm to be a working girl.'

CHAPTER FIVE

THIS February morn Jane accomplished her second trip to the north east with the eye of a veteran observing the landmarks with which she now felt herself to be familiar. There was still some snow on the Yorkshire moors but the month was obviously trying to establish its reputation as a fill-dyke seeing that low, grey clouds were being driven over the Pennines from the north west looming full of rain.

She felt easier in her mind about her godmother, having spent an entire day encouraging her to be thoroughly medically examined, X-rayed, blood-tested and the like. The immediate conclusions were that there was no sign of a tumour, either malignant or benign, which Jane had immediately feared. Though she had said that the symptoms could arise from fifty different causes, it was surprising how one was inclined to pessimism when—in one's greater knowledge—grim possibilities were omnipresent.

Still, she had left Aunt Irene (the 'aunt' being a courtesy title only) in the hands of an oculist and a neurologist. Between them she was sure they would find out the cause of the double vision and treat it.

Fortunately there was no need to worry about Elaine. Her mother was in very good health, indeed, and it was a pity she was seeing so much of Harry, who was not. What could be wrong with Harry, she fretted, with his attacks of tremor and self-impatience? He was growing more and more bad tempered and yet Elaine tolerated and excused him.

Possibly he was taking too much alcohol for one of his age and build, though he was the type of person who would resent advice which—to him—would be termed as interference with personal liberty.

She shrugged Harry away as not being her business and tried to anticipate the morrow, her first day as a qualified doctor doing the job for which she had studied since taking her 'A' level examinations. She had hated doing Greek; languages never having been her strong point, but Biology she had found fascinating to a degree and Chemistry an absolute playtime. Her father had bought her chemistry sets since she had ceased toddling and she had been quite knowledgeable on the subject before being required to take it up seriously.

She was looking forward tremendously to meeting Dr Potts again. Would she also never be allowed to open her mouth before him, as George had never done in her hearing? She wouldn't mind this very much since she would be there to listen to the opinions of others rather than air her own. Young housemen were rather like young fags; they were required to do as they were told without answering back and be there when they were required by their lords and masters. But the patients would talk to her. Bless them, they always did, sometimes when one hadn't time to listen to their woes or reminiscences or family histories.

She had been rather scared of real patients during her training when she had been required to act as a 'dresser' in either Outpatients or Casualty. Mostly they had blind faith in everyone concerned; even regarding a very vulnerable medical student as a lesser deity.

How could one ever live up to them and their belief in one's ability?

So she raced northwards torn between the natural confidence of youth and the doubts begotten by any new experience, but wholly committed and determined to live up to Hippocratic oath to the best of her considerable ability.

In the Hospital Administrator's office Jane watched the tropical fish swimming like so many jewels in the pellucid water. Did the fish belong to the hospital or the occupant of the room? she wondered. Who fed them? Were their lives as untrammelled as they appeared?

Having so far survived the bomb-blast of shock she asked, almost casually, 'How—er—how did he die, sir?'

'Cerebral haemorrhage,' Dr Fox answered her. 'It was not wholly unexpected. He had already survived two slight seizures last summer.'

'How dreadful,' Jane decided.

'Well that depends on whether one is the deceased or a survivor, Dr Pilgrim. He was roaring his way through his clinic when he decided to sit down and die. It was all over very quickly. You did not know him very well, of course, but we who did miss him considerably. But'—he shrugged—'we must go on.'

'Of—of course, sir,' Jane agreed. 'Does this—I mean—am I still—?'

'Dr Potts' death in no way affects your appointment, Dr Pilgrim. I hope you will loyally support the new consultant.'

'Of—of course, sir. I had better report for duty.'

Her head reeled as she left the Administrator's office. She might not have known Dr Potts for very long, but the impact he had had upon her was akin to a friendly steamroller. He must have been aware that there was a possibility of his sudden demise at any moment and yet he had seemed the very epitome of full and splendid life.

His doctors should never have allowed him to continue working, she mentally protested, and yet who could have stopped him doing anything to which he had made up his own mind?

Miss Pryce was sitting typing when Jane tapped and entered the consultant's office.

'Have—have you heard?' she whispered.

'Just now. Dr Fox told me. I was late arriving last evening, having missed my connection in Newcastle, so I had a meal in my room and went straight to bed. Nobody told me a thing.'

'I can't get over it,' Miss Pryce sniffed into an already damp handkerchief. 'He was there, joking away with a patient, when he turned to me and said: "Let's have a chair, love," and then he sort of toppled and—and looked funny. Dr Myers took the patient out and when he came back he said—said Doctor was dead.'

'Perhaps you shouldn't keep on thinking about it,' Jane said hastily. The dignity of death was always lost when other people tried to describe it. 'You have your work. That's always a great consolation.'

At that moment George Myers came in, nodding self-consciously towards the newcomer.

'Your first day, my last,' he said awkwardly, thus proving he was articulate. 'I'm not sorry, I can tell you.'

'You mean you're leaving, too?' Jane asked incredulously.

'What do you mean, "too"?' he joked heavily. 'I'm not leaving feet first, I hope, but my contract expires next week and I've landed a job near London where I can study for my Membership. They're letting me go in the circumstances because the new chief has his own assistant ready and waiting, so to speak.'

'He didn't choose *me*,' Jane said grimly. 'This new chief. He may not like me.'

'That's really quite irrelevant,' George Myers said

quietly. 'The less one's chief is made aware of one, the better. He isn't required to either like you or lump you. Providing you can tackle admissions with reasonable intelligence and compress all important information into a nutshell, he'll at least put up with you.'

'Thanks for the tip,' Jane smiled as the door opened and Richard Graves entered the room.

'Good morning, all!' he said formally. 'I see we're all ready for rounds.'

'You!' was torn from Jane. 'Are you the new—?'

It was not exactly the way to greet one's new chief, especially after the homily delivered by George Myers on the virtues of accepting one's role of utilitarian insignificance and keeping to it.

There was an electric silence which was broken by Dr Graves himself.

'With your permission, Doctor,' he said mockingly. 'You must excuse my obvious unsuitability for the part. A fellow feeling should inform you that we're both in the same boat. I, too, have yet to prove myself.'

'I—I'm sorry, sir. I didn't mean to—'

Dr Graves signalled to the resident, standing behind her. 'Dr Myers, could you go along and tell Sister I'll start my round in five minutes? Thank you. You—Miss—' he smiled at Miss Pryce. 'Could I have five minutes alone with my—er—colleague?'

'Certainly, Doctor.' It was obvious that Miss Pryce was already under the influence of a certain inherent charm which not only left Jane cold but antagonistic. When they were alone she said, awkwardly:

'If I sounded rude I'm sorry, sir. I was so surprised, you see.'

'I can't think why, Doctor. I am both suitably qualified and have been "shadowing" Dr Potts for some months, at his own request. If you were not acquainted with these facts it is an oversight with which I must not be accounted.'

He was being sarcastic and she hated him for it.

'Your name is Pilgrim, I believe?' he inquired, referring to some notes on the desk.

'Yes, sir.' Before he could comment she added hastily, 'My name seems to amuse many people. The same old jokes become boring with time.'

'I shall not joke about your name,' he promised her, 'seeing that *I* am similarly burdened.'

'Of course,' she pondered, 'with *his* name he should have been an undertaker!'

She quickly wondered if his use of the final word had been innocent or a deliberate pun, the product of a rapier-sharp mind. His well-bred secret smile as he scribbled answered her question and she wished she could have thought of something apt and clever with which to respond.

'Dr Pilgrim,' he now addressed her clearly, 'I may often prove unpopular in our future association but never—I hope—either unjust or unkind. Your career is as dear to me as it should be to yourself. I shall therefore expect you to observe a rigid discipline, obedience and a total disregard for the supposed limitations of your own body. I shall use the spur and provide the incentive; the rest is up to you.'

'I'll do my best, sir,' she said quietly.

'Good! I have three hospitals on my hands and a considerable private practice. Normally I will not have time for tête-à-têtes such as this has been. On the other hand I am always available for emergencies. I would rather my housemen shouted for help than drowned.'

He raised one quizzical eyebrow at her.

'He's too good-looking and too young,' she thought.

'He probably took all his exams in his stride. But one can't help respecting him.'

'Very good, sir,' she said aloud, and tagged on as he left the room and walked ahead of her to the medical wards.

'Observe,' he tossed over his shoulder at one point, 'and read up the patients for your first day or two. They're as good as the best thrillers and nobody can quite foresee how they're going to end.'

Jane found herself at the end of an impressive little procession as they entered the Women's Medical Ward. Dr Graves and Sister Godolphin went to either side of the first patient and Dr Myers took up his position next to the chief. A physiotherapist and an occupational therapist ranged either side of the foot of the bed with Jane in the middle, not quite knowing what she was supposed to do but keeping her eyes and ears open so that she would never feel quite so inadequate again.

The first patient was a victim of respiratory failure and in an oxygen tent. Her prognosis was not good and she was unconscious. The procession moved on rather quickly, not because it was lacking in feeling but knowing that it could do no more than was at present being done. The second patient was recovering from a secondary pneumonia, a living proof that modern drugs are stronger than the bacilli which cause these infections. So they went on round the ward; a renal failure here, an enlarged, painful gland there, an aneurysm, a growth, a bladder weakness and then Mrs MacBean.

Jane was to remember Mrs MacBean all her life.

'Observation, Doctor,' Sister announced, handing the consultant a file of notes which he rustled through quickly.

'Oh, yes,' he finally decided. 'I think we can hand Mrs MacBean to Dr Pilgrim for a day or two. You're not in any hurry to get home, are you, my dear?' he asked the patient.

'No, Doctor.' she answered lugubriously. 'Not as I am. I'm quite enjoying the rest.'

'Good! I want you to study Mrs MacBean's case, Dr Pilgrim,' he called out clearly to the rear of the party. 'I would rather you didn't see these notes. Play it the hard way, from scratch, and write up your findings. You should both enjoy that.'

He patted Mrs MacBean on her shoulder and strode on to the next and last bed. Jane found herself inattentive, which was very naughty of her. She looked back at Mrs MacBean, wondering how she would make out with what was obviously a test case of her ability to diagnose. The woman had once been pretty though she was now far too plump. She was already nodding off to sleep as though she had endured a wakeful night.

Suddenly aware that everyone was looking at her, Jane jumped to attention.

'Sir?' she said automatically.

'Oh, so you're with us again,' Richard Graves said sharply. 'Brown studies must only be indulged in your limited spare time, Dr Pilgrim.'

Jane almost retorted hotly as she flushed crimson. A public reprimand was one of the most difficult things to bear with any grace.

'Sorry, sir,' she forced herself to say through her humiliation.

The round went on. The men were visited and then the patients in the private wing. After this the Consultant's instructions were carried out; a drip was erected here and an intravenous injection given there. One elderly man went suddenly and unaccountably into heart failure and had to be resuscitated. There were three new admissions to be installed as this was the season of chills;

two were virus pneumonias and the other a chronic bronchitis.

On legs which felt like india rubber Jane found herself in the doctors' dining room tackling cool cod liberally bespattered with lumpy parsley sauce. She hadn't had time to talk with Mrs MacBean yet but hoped she would have some opportunity during the afternoon.

One thing was sharply clear in her mind, however. It was a conclusion she had already confided to Olga and now it was brought home to her yet again. The dead so quickly became horrifyingly unimportant. Only when this fact was realised and acknowledged could a busy hospital continue so efficiently to serve the living.

This morning she had bitterly resented the man who had stepped into another's shoes, but by lunch time she was a willing member of his team and eagerly awaiting any accolades he might care to bestow on her during the course of her somewhat tortuous progress.

CHAPTER SIX

FITTING in her chats and examinations of Mrs MacBean whenever she had a spare moment, which wasn't often, Jane gradually built up a physical picture and drew her own conclusions. It wasn't easy because the woman's symptoms were all inconclusive in themselves. She had gradually begun to feel tired during the course of her household duties so had taken to resting in the afternoons. For this she blamed the increase in her weight which she bitterly regretted.

'My own doctor put me on a diet,' she explained, 'but I was terribly disappointed when I lost only ounces. My husband joined me in my diet, to make things easier, and he lost half a stone in the same time.'

'And you're sure you didn't cheat?' Jane asked, adding with a smile: 'It's so easy. The extra slice of bread, the biscuit with a cup of tea . . .'

'No, I did not,' said Mrs MacBean, sharply. 'They all suggest that. But I kept to the diet and I might as well not have bothered.'

'Don't be discouraged,' Jane quickly urged. 'I take it it's a general lassitude which really troubles you?'

'That's right. I'm always tired. That and my bad temper. My husband says I've even got a bad tempered face.'

Jane began to feel a little excited.

'And you haven't always been like this?' she asked.

'No. I was as placid as could be at one time. Lying here I feel almost like my old self. But I can't spend my life in bed when there's nothing really wrong with me, can I?'

49

'Oh, there's something wrong with you,' Jane assured her, 'and I'm beginning to think I know what it is. I'm sure Dr Graves does already. Don't worry. We'll put you right.'

Jane wrote out her conclusions after careful examination.

'Mrs MacBean complains of general lassitude. She has difficulty in controlling her weight, despite dieting, and her skin is dry in places, particularly on her legs. She has also suffered a personality change and there is an inclination for her features to have coarsened. (I have seen a photograph taken of her five years ago and can confirm this.) Her hair is quite good but her eyebrows are thin and poor. She assures me she hasn't plucked them for months. Her fingers are inclined to be spatulate and she shows all the signs of being a sub-thyroid subject which could deteriorate into myxodoema unless treated promptly.'

Feeling rather proud of herself for having spotted something of which she had only previously read, Jane had the Senior Pathologist, Dr Waddell, make a blood test to confirm her diagnosis of sub-thyroidism.

His findings reached her early the same evening. She stared disbelievingly at the statement that there was nothing in the sample of Mrs MacBean's blood to confirm her suggestion of lack of thyroid.

She felt suddenly depressed and wondered if she had been guilty of building her conclusions on too little evidence.

She was in the Ward Office at the time and started as Richard Graves entered.

'Good evening, Dr Pilgrim!' he greeted her.

'Good evening, sir. I—I didn't know you were in the building.'

'I just dropped in.' He shrugged this off. 'I believe

you have been doing a bit of detective work on Mrs MacBean?'

'Yes, I have, sir. But I'm sorry to say I haven't got very far. My theory has just been exploded by the path people.'

She handed him both her typed statement and the chitty from Dr Waddell, which he studied attentively.

'The very devil, isn't it?' he asked her with a smile. 'But don't worry. I came to exactly the same conclusion.'

'You did, sir?' she felt relieved. 'Then you were wrong, too.'

'I wouldn't say that,' he charmingly corrected her. 'One lives and learns. If we could fit our diagnoses, along with path reports, into a perfect jigsaw, it would all be too easy. But quite often physical signs and pathological specimens fail to agree. As with our Mrs MacBean. She is a typical thyroid. Her irritability, lassitude, increased weight, dry skin and partial loss of hair from the brows are all signs of thyroid deficiency, and though I do not agree that she would develop into a chronic myxodoema I do agree that she is not very happy with her lot at the present time. The deficiency is not evident in her blood. Don't let that put you off. I suggest we treat this woman as a borderline case of sub-thyroidism. The dosage to commence with will be correspondingly small. We'll keep her in and give her half a grain once daily for a week. If there are no side effects we'll discharge her and increase the dose to two half grains daily for a further two weeks, and so on. Borderline or not, I wouldn't be at all surprised to find her absorbing four grains daily after six months. So I'll still leave our problem patient with you, Doctor. Don't promise her the earth, but if she isn't feeling a little more lively by this time next week I'll cheerfully eat my hat.'

'Thank you, sir, that's most encouraging,' she

dimpled at him. 'And I certainly hope you don't have to do it.'

He regarded her for a moment, deciding she was an autumn leaf of a girl with her golden brown bright hair and matching eyes. Without allowing his thoughts to show he said offhandedly: 'Dr Forrester will be commencing duty tomorrow. You have done very well to manage for a couple of days virtually on your own. Well done!'

'There was Dr Fox to call on, sir,' she admitted. 'And you have been in each evening.'

'I think you should meet Dr Forrester for an informal chat,' he suddenly suggested. 'There never seems time in the rush of the day to get to know one another. This is my address,' he thrust a card into her surprised hands. 'Come to dinner at eight o'clock and meet her then.'

She had barely thanked him before he turned to rush off somewhere else, telling her he could find his own way out.

So the new registrar was another woman! She supposed she could scarcely refuse an invitation issued by her chief, though it was somewhat nerve-racking to be asked to meet another woman doctor on his premises.

She hoped Dr Forrester was elderly and efficient.

Why should she be remotely interested in what her immediate superior was like as a woman? she questioned herself. Because she was more experienced did not necessarily mean that she was hag-ridden.

She was conscious of the young professional woman's reluctance to work under another woman.

'Which is all wrong,' she chided herself. 'I should be glad and proud that women are holding down responsible positions once denied them.'

Sister Godolphin interrupted this brief period of self analysis by reclaiming her office.

'So it's you, Dr Pilgrim,' she said maternally. She was a large, buxom woman with a big heart. 'Did you get any tea?'

'Well—er—Sister—'

'That means you didn't,' Sister sighed. 'I won't have my doctors neglecting themselves. Now go down to the canteen this instant and have a cup of tea and a chocolate biscuit. There's a lot of energy in chocolate.'

Jane went off obediently after giving instructions regarding Mrs MacBean's treatment. She was finding that hospital sisters were a very mixed bunch, indeed, and that whereas Sister Godolphin was always driving her off in search of some refreshment or other, Sister Frear, who was in charge of Men's Medical, was always sending for her when she was either in the middle of a meal or about to go off duty. Even though she had been in the ward only five minutes earlier, Sister would find someone about whom she was worried or something which needed to be done at the most inconvenient times.

Sister Weller, who was in charge of the Private Patients' Wing, was young, pretty and the worst hypochondriac Jane had ever known. She reflected every new admission's symptoms until someone came in with a new lot. She seemed to spend her entire existence fearing dire possibilities instead of appreciating the good health she really enjoyed, and each time Jane saw her she had to be reassured on yet a different score.

On this evening Jane was off duty promptly at six, thanks to Sister Frear enjoying thirty-six hours' freedom from the hospital and her staff nurse being much more considerate of housemen, and so she went to her room to look out a dress which would be fitting for a dinner with one's consultant chief and yet not too elaborate.

One of her new dresses was ideal for the occasion. It

was a heavy green silk crépe, with a softly pleated skirt and a tie-neck. Jane's colouring was always complemented by green, and when she had taken a bath and dressed up she was well pleased with the general effect. She hoped she might chance wearing high heeled shoes and would have to risk being called out on another emergency involving a scramble down a ravine.

Already there was a certain comradeship between herself and the hospital's other housemen; one of them, Andrew Laurie, had made the offer of the use of his car whenever he was not using it himself. As she knew he was on call this evening she asked if she might borrow the car and was told all would be in order and that the keys would be left at the Night Porter's desk. Andrew would not hear of her paying for the loan, so she determined to at least have the petrol tank filled to capacity as a token of her appreciation.

At half past seven she ventured forth in the old Mini; not being very familiar with either the car or the district and wanting to give herself plenty of time to find Dr Graves' house. This was a truly gracious residence called Hadrian's Retreat. Apparently the Scots had succeeded in driving the Romans back until they had dug in and built another portion of their famous wall. There are many signs of this famous rampart all across the unspoilt border country between England and Scotland, but on this particular evening Jane did not know of the Roman well in Richard Graves' garden or the barrow which adjoined his property. She would not have been scared by the proximity of Roman bones but she might well have been impressed by the information.

A housekeeper admitted her to the warm, well kept house and she was shown into a pleasant room where a log fire roared and sent up licks of flame which reflected in golden oak parquet flooring and panelling.

She had scarcely seated herself, with the current edition of the *BMJ*, than her host came to greet her.

'A truly wonderful guest, Dr Pilgrim,' he told her, after a brief glance which summed up her appearance and approved it, thus making her thrill unaccountably and for the first time regard her superior as a man rather than a knowledgeable physician. 'You delight my staff by arriving for a meal in time to have an apéritif and still not cause the potatoes to be charred. You will be welcome again. But no doubt Dr Forrester will claim her usual prerogative and keep both us thoughtful characters waiting. What will you have, Dr Pilgrim?'

'I would like a sherry, please. Dry, if you have it.'

He poured two glasses of sherry and handed her one with a courtly little bow.

'Now we come to the vexed question,' he smiled after he had replenished the glasses. 'Having drunk together things can never be quite so formal between us again. I hope I may be allowed to call you Jane?'

'Yes—er—certainly.' She was flushed and the wine was warming, but she knew better than to leap into familiarities with him. He was still very much the boss of her outfit even though he might be inclined to relax at this moment before his own hearth.

'Now there's a pretty name,' he went on conversationally. 'Nothing plain about a name like Jane.'

She wanted to say that Richard was a nice name, too, but she forbore. This was not a mutual admiration society and she was probably being expertly sized up at this very moment.

She was relieved when he was called away to answer the 'phone, having time to wonder how she was standing up to the test and somehow minding how he felt about having her thrust on his staff. She realised that he was off duty and being charming, but this did not mean that he would excuse any lack of either attention or efficiency in her during tomorrow's round.

He returned to say, with what she thought to be a regretful air, that Dr Forrester had been unavoidably delayed and might not be able to come at all that evening.

'So we must dine tête-à-tête, Jane,' he said with a small, crooked smile. 'It is too bad, and you will probably believe that I arranged it all.'

'Not at all, sir,' she decided to humour him. 'I am a doctor's daughter and know from personal experience how difficult it is to arrange a social occasion where everybody both turns up and stays to the end. I think it has happened about once in my home.'

'Ralph Pilgrim?' he queried.

'Yes, sir. He was my father.'

'So you are *that* Pilgrim's daughter, eh? It has been teasing me who it was you resembled. He was a fine-looking man, your father.'

'Yes, I was very proud of him.'

'And he of you, no doubt, that you decided to follow in his footsteps.'

'The first ones, at least,' she sighed. 'I don't suppose I shall ever reach my father's eminence.'

'Why not, if you're so minded? Or perhaps you'll be distracted by marriage. Women usually are.'

'Oh, I don't think I would allow marriage to distract *me*,' Jane said promptly. 'It would have to fit in with my other plans, not supersede them.'

'Obviously you are not in love, Jane.'

'How can you be so sure of that, sir?' she asked, flushing.

'Because a woman in love finds arguments which permit her to keep her career as a second string to marriage, not the other way round. If one must be sacrificed then it is unequivocally the career.'

'What a waste!' Jane said, shocked.

'Yes. But then some husbands are very understanding about this knotty problem and yours may be one of them. I will hope so. Shall we go in to dinner?'

He offered her his arm and together they walked across the hall and into the dining room where candles played their soft light in the dark red of a fine mahogany refectory table. There were two places set, one at either end.

'I think we'll move you up here, Jane,' he said, carrying silver and crystal with a total disregard for its safety and setting it on the right of the table next to his own place at the head. 'I do so hate dodging the impedimenta when I am trying to see my guest. Are you comfortable? My dining chairs are an abomination to all my friends and I must go shopping for new ones one of these days. Perhaps Lyn would advise me. She is always trying to persuade me to modernise my effects.'

Jane pondered that 'Lyn' must be Dr Forrester and that when she modernised his effects she might well be Mrs Graves. She hoped, somewhat arbitrarily, that this event would not take place during her stay with the 'firm'.

CHAPTER SEVEN

ALTHOUGH Jane had not intended allowing the promised
tête-à-tête to become a heart-to-heart, she found herself
confiding easily in the somewhat stern faced man sitting
at her elbow. This may have been accounted to the wine;
firstly they enjoyed a palate-tingling hock and later a
very smooth Beaune with the roast beef; but it was not
the first time that Jane had taken wine with a meal,
though Northingham Infirmary did not run to such
luxuries for its residents.

She found herself confiding her hopes and fears,
telling of Elaine's somewhat giddy existence since her
father's death and her own sense of responsibility in the
matter.

'Sometimes I think *I* am her mother,' she smiled
somewhat apologetically. 'But what do you want to
know about *my* problems? I'm sorry, sir. You should
have stopped me.'

'Not at all. My housemen's problems are automatically mine. Mostly these turn out to be unsuitable or
ambitious young women,' he smiled, 'but yours is a gay
and pretty mama. How refreshing! Perhaps she is not,
after all, your responsibility. You may, in her opinion,
be concerning yourself in something which is no longer
your business. I'm sure she can well cope with any
eventuality despite the air of incompetence she no doubt
assumes for your benefit.'

'Oh!' Jane said sharply. 'I see what you mean. It looks
to you as though I should let her go her own way, making
her own mistakes, while I go mine. Is that it? I shouldn't

mind if she marries Harry and makes a mess of her life?'

'Now don't be naughty and petulant, Jane!' She felt about six years old as he chided her. 'Unless you are prepared to allow your mother to choose your husband you must grant her the right to choose hers. She managed once without your consent and I'm sure she's quite capable of doing so again. We'll have coffee in the library, shall we? It's much cosier in there.'

The library lent itself to talk on medicine for its walls were lined with text books.

'Poverty is usually the houseman's bane,' he said blandly, 'so my housekeeper is instructed to allow any member of my staff to come here and study at will. I hope you will take advantage of this, Jane. I suppose you will wish to better yourself professionally?'

'Oh, yes, sir. I would like to shut myself in with books for hours.'

'Within reason,' he smiled. 'You also need to play. You're young, pretty and there's spring just around the corner. That usually plays havoc with all one's good intentions.'

'You, too, sir?' she suddenly inquired daringly. He looked at her as though not quite believing her temerity and she flushed as she stumbled on: 'What I meant was that you, too, sir, are apparently young enough to be affected by the spring. You're much younger than Dr Potts, that is. I—I—didn't mean to be impertinent.' Her voice died in a well of embarrassment.

'You haven't been impertinent in the least, Jane. You simply startled me by stating the bald truth. I suppose I am young enough for such delights but age doesn't always count. I seem to have been bowed down under responsibility for years. Perhaps that is why I showed a desire to champion your mother's airy independence. I secretly envy her. Yes?' he called as a tap came upon the door.

'May I come in, Uncle Ricky?'

'One of my heaviest responsibilities,' he told Jane ruefully, 'is a rebellious, teenage ward. Come in, Griselda!' he called in a louder tone.

The heavy door opened and in came one of the most beautiful creatures Jane had ever seen. It was almost too obvious that she was related to Richard Graves; they both shared the same patrician features and dark, smooth hair; but whereas his eyes were a clear, steel grey, the girl's were sepia and soulful. She was about sixteen and her woman's body was enveloped in a tailored silk dressing gown. She also wore too much make-up, as though she had been spending the past hour endeavouring to paint the lily she undoubtedly was.

Richard Graves made the introductions.

'Dr Pilgrim, this is my niece and ward, Griselda Rayne; Griselda, my houseman at Northingham, Jane Pilgrim.'

'Another woman doctor?' Griselda pondered after how d'you do's had been murmured. 'I'll bet Lyn doesn't like that. Have you asked her, Uncle Ricky?'

'Whatever are you talking about? Now say goodnight and get off to bed. It's back to school for you in the morning.'

'Oh, Uncle! Do I have to? Can't I try to make a go of a career? I promise to go back to school if I make a mess of it. Honestly!'

'Please say goodnight, Griselda.' The voice was suddenly as cold and forbidding as ice.

'Oh, all right. Goodnight, Dr Pilgrim!'

The girl flounced out without another word and Jane wished heartily that she hadn't witnessed what was obviously a painful domestic scene.

'In case you are thinking I give advice without being prepared to take it,' he said heavily, 'my niece has taken french leave from school, at a time when she should be studying for exams, with a view to taking up modelling as a career. She thinks that all she needs are her natural assets and that modelling is the most superb of careers. She is at St Etheldreda's, and I have practically had to go on my knees to persuade her headmistress to take her back again. I have only to imagine Griselda in some big city, alone apart from her "modelling" friends, to give myself nightmares. And you dared to suggest that I might be considered young!'

'She's at a difficult age,' Jane sympathised. 'Girls turn to their mothers, or some woman, as a rule when they're growing up. I suppose women better understand their problems and ambitions. Griselda finds you harsh and unsympathetic whereas you're acting only for her good. Every girl goes through a stage when she wants to do, or be, something beautiful. Modelling, the stage, dancing; they all appeal to the feminine in us. It's a temporary phase but it does need understanding.'

'Are you telling me I should have let her go ahead and model, Jane?'

'No, of course not,' she laughed. 'You might have said, "Well, we'll see how you do in your exams and then talk it over." I'm sure she would come to you with a different ambition by then.'

'Probably going from the ridiculous to the sublime she would decide she wanted to be the next woman astronaut, with full honours in maths and bio-chemistry to justify her claim.'

'And then you would feel pangs at turning her loose among the stars,' Jane said slyly. 'If it is true that a daughter has no right to interfere with her mother's freedom of action, it is surely even more true that the young, when fledged, must be allowed to fly away. I think you are resisting that truth, sir.'

'Perhaps you're right,' he sighed. 'I can't bear to think of Griselda ever getting hurt. And yet I may be the one who is really hurting her. You're a wise little Pilgrim, Jane. I'm glad of this chat. I'll tell my niece, tomorrow, that a little more leaning can only improve her vital statistics.'

They smiled at one another, liking one another and feeling drawn together by the similitude of so many of their views. Their cosy intercourse was interrupted for the second time, however, by a much more disturbing presence. All at once of three, Jane was the third, when Lyn Forrester decided to turn up at Hadrian's Retreat for a drink and a chat.

'Sorry I couldn't manage dinner, Ricky,' she said easily, absorbing him with two china blue eyes fringed by long, silken lashes. Her hair was a golden cap and her complexion milky. She looked fragile and her figure was Dresden-like and exquisite. She couldn't have been less than twenty-eight, allowing for her qualifications, but she looked much younger without having to try. 'I was having trouble with Nigel. I think I'm going to have to talk to you about him'—she bit her lip—'but obviously it must be some other time.' She smiled brightly around her. 'You must be Dr Pilgrim,' she decided. 'Ricky, introduce us, you old slowcoach!'

By this time Jane had decided that Dr Forrester was their host's familiar. In the short time she had been in the house she had somehow contrived to make this very clear. Now she turned to him and asked: 'May I go up and see my favourite teenager for a moment, or is she in dire disgrace?'

'In disgrace, but not dire. Of course you may see her, Lyn. She was disappointed when I told her you might not be able to come. I'll order more coffee, so don't be too long.'

Jane felt awkward when the other had gone upstairs. She didn't understand why she should feel that the evening had unaccountably deteriorated. There was no sign other than that Richard Graves was delighted by his colleague's belated arrival. He ordered the coffee, ferreted out a third brandy glass and generally prepared to enjoy the company.

Drawing on a cigar he said casually: 'Dr Forrester is a widow, you know.'

'Is she?' Jane asked. 'No, I didn't know.'

'She has four-year-old twins, Nigel and Carmel. The boy is rather delicate. He has a hole in his heart.'

'Oh! I'm sorry to hear that. It must be very worrying to have sick children.'

'It is. I think Lyn keeps up remarkably well. You wouldn't think she had a care in the world most of the time.'

Jane felt suddenly ashamed of herself. She had been prepared to be antagonistic towards Dr Forrester purely by instinct. That 'taking charge of the situation' attitude of the newcomer's had evolved because she had been required to 'take charge' of her own situations or go under.'

When she returned to the library, just after the coffee arrived, Jane deliberately tried to feel more charitable towards her.

'By the way,' Lyn said, after observing that it was after ten o'clock, 'are you familiar with the district, Dr Pilgrim? It's a stinking night. There's a thick mist cutting visibility down to ten yards in parts. Haven't you to be in by eleven? I know I had when I was a house-surgeon. It doesn't do to break rules during one's first week, does it? I only live a few minutes away by car and I know the way blindfold by now. I should do, shouldn't I, darling?' she asked their host.

'I—I think I should be going,' Jane said uncertainly.

'I'd forgotten about that silly rule,' said Dr Graves. 'I'll run you back.'

'No, thanks. I have a car. A borrowed car. I'm sure if it's a bad night the owner will be glad to see it back safe and sound.' Jane paused by Lyn Forrester's chair. 'I suppose we'll meet tomorrow, Dr Forrester?'

'Yes, my dear.' The other smiled with everything but her doll-like eyes. 'I hope you don't find me an ogre, but I shall be a terrible task master.'

'I hope I shan't prove a terrible pupil.'

'Both of us will judge and be judged in due course, no doubt.'

It was only when Jane was driving through a perfectly normal drizzle that she realised she had practically been told to go away and had gone. Lyn Forrester had obviously decided that she was *de trop* and yet her removal of the unwanted guest had been accomplished with the utmost finesse.

When Jane eventually reported in at the hospital she was informed that the eleven o'clock rule only applied to those residents who were on night call, and she was not.

'You can stay out all night if you want, Doctor,' the night porter said cheerfully.

'No, thanks,' smiled Jane. 'The night life in Northingham isn't so very hectic and there's always tomorrow to think about. I can't think of a better place to go to than bed.'

But it was well after midnight before her thoughts would allow her to sleep, and even after that her dreams were troubled by rebellious, beautiful girls and sickly children and a fiercely spitting wild animal which had very blue eyes and lethal claws menacing her.

CHAPTER EIGHT

THE next day Jane was forced to admit to herself that she had obviously been prejudiced against Dr Forrester merely by instinct.

The Registrar could not have been kinder or more tolerant, and as Jane experienced one of those days when everything seemed determined to go wrong with her from the start, she certainly appreciated the tolerance of her immediate superior.

As it was not the day for the Consultant's visit they did the round together, this time accompanied only by the Ward Sister instead of the usual procession. Lyn was kindness itself with the patients who were very ill but inclined to skip quickly past those who were either on the road to recovery or ready for discharge.

'Dr Pilgrim will come back and have a word with you later,' she said frequently. 'I'm rather busy.'

Thus Jane was made doubly busy and missed her morning coffee as well as being late for lunch.

'You must keep to a timetable, Doctor,' Sister Godolphin chided her that afternoon as she was seeing to a woman admission. 'Dr Forrester had no right to skip the round like that and put it on to you. Dr Myers never neglected seeing every patient every day. It breaks the monotony for the poor dears, well or ill.'

'Oh, I didn't mind,' Jane smiled. 'It's all experience, Sister. I certainly need all of that I can get. I knew Dr Forrester had an important luncheon engagement.'

Sister made a rude, deprecatory noise.

'We could all have appointments at the expense of doing our duty,' she said acidly.

Jane concluded, in some amusement, that Dr Forrester's glamorous good looks set the nursing staff against her rather than the reverse. They probably concluded, as she had done herself, that it was only a matter of time before Dr Forrester became Mrs Dr Graves, and this would mean disappointment to many of the hospital's romantically minded nurses who saw in Richard Graves the ideal husband for themselves.

Along with receiving new admissions and advising those to be discharged about their further treatment, if any, at the Outpatients' clinics, Jane studied the case histories of all her patients and wrote her own reports for Richard Graves to see. As the days passed she found herself seeing less and less of him on the days he attended the hospital. She didn't notice how cleverly Lyn edged her away from him; sending her on an errand here or there or asking her to do something at a moment's notice.

'Will you put up a drip for Mr Samuels in the Private Wing, dear?' the Registrar requested one day.

'Certainly. May I leave it until after the round? I missed most of it on Friday.'

'I think we can manage without you for the round, dear, and the drip is rather urgent. Perhaps I should do it and you take the round?'

'Oh, no!' Jane demurred. 'I didn't mean to imply that I wouldn't do it, Doctor. I'll go right away.'

Sister Frear, however, was firmly of the opinion that the business should wait until after rounds.

'This man has antibodies in his blood,' she snapped, 'and the path people aren't sure he should be transfused until they make further investigations. Mr Samuels has stopped vomiting and there's less risk of dehydration.

We'll leave it until Dr Graves has seen him.'

Naturally Jane sped back to the female ward and tagged on to the end of the procession, which had reached the third bed. She didn't notice the glance of surprised fury which Lyn Forrester darted at her.

'Oh! Dr Pilgrim'—said Richard Graves, though she could have sworn he hadn't even noticed her, so unobtrusive had been her arrival—'I was wondering where you had got to. Let me know if our itinerary interferes with your other activities.' Jane flushed pink and she almost allowed a hot retort to leave her lips before the discipline of years sealed them. 'Come here and listen to this.'

She obediently took out her own stethoscope and placed it against the patient's exposed chest. The normal, cheerful *ba-rum*, *ba-rum* of the human heart beat was in this case marred by a faint hiss, as though there was air in the heart's chambers.

Jane looked up at the consultant, wondering what he wished her to say in front of the patient.

'Tell Mrs Reid what you hear,' he invited cordially.

'There's a decided murmur, sir.'

'I'll say,' he agreed. 'It's like a pair of bellows in there. Our dear Mrs Reid has been working five days a week in a laundry despite that little lot, and it was only after she almost fainted into the bleach that her doctor persuaded her to come to us for a rest. Which proves,' he told the assembly philosophically, 'that you're never dead until you actually lie down and admit it. Mrs Reid will probably still be refusing to admit it long after she's ninety.'

They moved on and eventually reached Mrs MacBean who was awaiting notice of discharge. She was responding very well to additional thyroid treatment and felt much better with a regenerated outlook on life.

'You must be faithful in your dieting,' the consultant

told her after advising both her and Sister that she could leave the following morning. 'You'll find it extremely difficult to lose the extra weight you are already carrying, without adding more. The sub-thyroid subject hangs on to fat like a miser to his gold. But persevere. If you live within smelling distance of a fried fish and chip shop, move house.'

Everyone laughed in high good humour. Dr Graves was certainly enjoying his round today.

In the corridor between Women's and Men's wards Dr Forrester sidled near her junior.

'What about that drip?' she demanded.

'Sister wanted to wait for the chief. She said the path people had found antibodies and that the man was improving in any case.'

'Does Sister give you your instructions or I?' the other said coldly. 'Really, Jane, this is too bad of you!'

Jane flushed under the reprimand as the other slid into step once more beside the consultant. Apparently she was fated to be unpopular with somebody no matter whom she tried to please.

She felt doubly guilty as Richard Graves examined the Pathologist's report on Mr Samuels in Sister's office, and then gave his views firmly.

'He could take a couple of pints of saline without any risk whatsoever,' he advocated. 'This should have been done pending my arrival. The poor fellow's practically mummified. See to it immediately, Dr Pilgrim. We'll excuse you the rest of the round.'

Jane felt the daggers drawn between Sister Frear and the Registrar were finding their marks in her own tender flesh as she stood like a buffer between them.

Jane soon discovered that Dr Forrester was not averse to a gossip whenever they were together and she particularly enjoyed speaking of her children.

'They're a blessing,' she admitted. 'Though an awful responsibility at times. But for them I have come to the conclusion that early marriage is a mistake in professional women. Don't you be tempted, my dear.'

'I have no plans for marriage whatsoever.'

'Wise girl. I thought I could have my cake and eat it, but there's only one way of having children and my precious career was the sacrifice to motherhood. After Jon died I don't think I would ever have scrambled back into the game if Richard hadn't sponsored me. He gave me a job as his assistant while I looked round and then backed me when I applied for this post. My mother looks after the twins for me and I get home every weekend. It's all working out quite well, really.'

'I'm glad.'

'You're a sweet, sympathetic child, Jane. Of course, my social life's a bit limited as dear Richard is always complaining. I have to let Mother off the leash at weekends and it's so difficult to get baby sitters, especially with Nigel as he is. Nobody likes the responsibility and he's a spoilt child, of course. Invalid children always are.'

'Could I help?' Jane quickly offered. 'I adore children.'

'You amaze me,' Lyn admitted. 'I can't say that about other people's children. I find my own a tie. But it would be wonderful if I could count on you now and again. When are you free?'

'Every other Saturday I'm off duty at seven. I'm free this week. I was going to accept the chief's offer of using his library, but that can wait.'

'You mean he told you to go there whenever you liked?' Lyn asked quickly. 'I shouldn't take that invitation too literally. Richard's a darling, but his housekeeper hates people dropping in informally. She's the type who follows you with a duster and expects you to have slippers to change into. Of course one can't complain to Richard that she puts one off.'

'I see,' Jane said, disappointed when she thought of all that library of wonderful text books going to waste. 'Well, can I relieve you on Saturday?'

'You're too kind,' Lyn effused, but took advantage of that kindness with alacrity. 'I hope I can do you a favour in return sometime. By the way, Richard—I suppose I should remember to call him Dr Graves in front of you—wishes you to stand in with him at the clinic on Tuesday afternoons. I should have remembered to tell you yesterday because now it leaves you so little time to read up the patients' notes. You'll find them with Sister Outpatients and she doesn't allow anything to leave her office. Really, these sisters are the very limit sometimes. However, do your best.'

Jane found that by skipping her tea period and staying late in the Outpatients department she had time to make a cursory assessment of the patients' notes for the morrow's clinic. It did not occur to her to chide her colleague for having failed to inform her earlier that she would be required to attend at yet another medical adventure. Dr Forrester had quite enough on her plate with one thing and another, she excused her.

That evening she found herself sitting at supper by Colin Oundle, the ENT junior.

'How about a swap?' Colin asked her. 'Have you any leanings towards ENT?'

'Not at all. I associate it with horrid little instruments in horribly confined places. If I must be a surgeon I'll choose the abdomen for my field of operation. Why do you suddenly want to swap? Sick of your own job?'

'My dear kid, have you seen *my* chief? He's a positive

Hyde to everybody but his private patients. As a female you're a dead loss to your firm.'

'I beg your pardon! Female or not I do my stint.'

'Now keep your pretty brown hair on. I meant you're wasted with Dr Forrester. You can't possibly adore her as I do.'

'Oh, I see!' smiled Jane. 'Yes, she is attractive.'

'That's not exactly what I meant. You, dear girl, are attractive, but she has a way of tossing one a glance with RSVP written all over it. She's looked at me so once or twice and I would like to take her up on it. But def!'

'You're mistaken,' Jane teased, still noting that Colin was the Adonis of the housemen with his leonine head and fair complexion. 'I'm sure she's bespoken by a bigger gun than you'll ever be!'

'No kidding! I shall shoot myself. Actually I didn't intend to offer her the protection of my name. I don't think that's what she's expecting of yours truly—quite.'

'I'm sure it's all in your imagination,' Jane said firmly. 'And anyway, you should be far too busy for such nonsense, like me.'

CHAPTER NINE

THE Outpatients and Casualty block were new buildings attached to the Victorian monstrosity which was Northingham Infirmary. The Management Committee were very proud of this addition with its shining pastel paints and modern rubberised flooring and chromium fittings and floral decor; not to mention the cafeteria and the cubicle doors marching down the wide, spacious corridors, each one finished in a different colour to bring cheer to the hearts and eyes of those who came depressed with sickness to see the specialists.

Jane had been briefed by Dr Graves for a few minutes after his arrival. She was to see a few old and chronic patients and use her common sense.

'I always see new patients myself,' he explained. 'Don't try to handle anything you can't manage and I'm only next door if you want me.'

He appeared somewhat reserved this afternoon, but Jane forgot this as she looked round her small consulting room, which was painted sunshine yellow and had a lavender door.

By her elbow were six folders containing the case-histories of the patients she was to see. The first was a Mr Hetherington and the last entry in his notes was signed by Richard Graves.

'Query disseminated sclerosis?' (he had written). 'Signs and symptoms extremely slight and dubious. Will see again in one month.'

Jane closed the folder, for nothing was intentionally revealed to a patient during the exploratory stages of his troubles, and looked up, smiling, as the duty nurse showed Mr Hetherington into the cubicle. He was a farmer type of person, large and well built. He was also a man of some reticence.

'Now, Mr Hetherington,' Jane said cheerfully. 'Tell me about yourself.'

'Eh?' he asked somewhat aggressively. 'I already told you other doctor last time I came.'

'But you didn't tell *me*,' she sighed. 'I would really like to know.'

'I ought to be ploughing,' he said crossly. 'An' not wasting my time 'ere.'

'But now that you *are* here, what's wrong?'

'Don't you know yet?' he demanded. 'You've 'ad a month to find out.'

'Well has anything got worse since then?' she almost pleaded, trying a new tack. 'You were finding it difficult to grasp things. Remember?'

'Of course I remember. It was happening to me, hinny. My, but you're young! When policemen and school teachers and doctors begin to look like lads and lasses, folk like me are getting old.'

'*I'll* be a lot older by tonight, Mr Hetherington, if you refuse to talk to me.' Jane sighed in exasperation. 'I *am* a doctor but a very junior one. My chief will think I'm helpless if we don't have something to show for your visit. Of course, it you'd rather see him . . . ?' she hesitated and the man relented.

'Well, there's not much more to tell, only that it's so damned awkward in my job, begging your pardon! I reach out to do summat, like switching the milking machine on, and my ruddy 'and starts to shake like in a palsy. The other day I couldn't change gear on the tractor until I'd near gone in the drainage ditch. Last night my beer shot straight out o' my 'and, and there was

I dithering like a dotard in the public bar.'

A distant remembrance stirred at the back of Jane's mind.

'Do you take much alcohol, Mr Hetherington?' she asked.

'A couple of pints of light ale most nights is my limit. The wife only keeps cider in the house. It's not the DTs I've damned well got!' he decided aggressively.

'No, I'm not suggesting you have,' Jane said, quickly, putting the remembrance she was seeking quickly aside. 'Let us see if we can find out what's wrong. This little hammer—you may have seen one before—we use to test nervous reactions in limbs. I'm going to put it down in different places on the desk and you are going to pick it up and give it back to me. We'll do it all very quickly.'

Three times the man returned the hammer to her without difficulty; at the fourth attempt, however, he failed to grasp it and his hand shook as though with a sudden ague.

'Damn it!' he said angrily, and took it in his left hand and stilled it, like a frightened bird.

'Don't worry,' Jane said quickly, though she was feeling far too worried for her own comfort. 'It is only your right hand which plays this trick, I gather?'

'As I'm right 'anded that's precious little comfort,' the man decided.

'Just stay there a moment. I'll have a word with Dr Graves about you,' Jane decided.

The nurse stepped into the consulting room while Jane tapped on the door next to her own.

'Trouble already?' Richard Graves asked kindly, turning from the patient he was examining.

'Well, it's Mr Hetherington, sir. Here are his notes. I haven't seen one, you see, sir,' she pointed out his queried diagnosis, 'and I'm afraid it is. Doesn't it begin with—with *intention tremor*?' The other nodded. 'Well, it seems to have become worse since he was here last. He almost had an accident with his tractor because he couldn't change gear. I'm worried about him, sir.'

'You're not here to worry about them,' he said quietly. 'Only to treat and advise them, Dr Pilgrim. You may find a bronchiectasis which becomes a fulminating pneumonia within hours, or an accepted lumbago which turns out to be a carcinoma of the spine. You can't worry about these things. That's not a doctor's job. They're as cute as monkeys,' he went on in a gentler tone, 'and they can scent your worry. *I'll* see Mr Hetherington after Mrs Dacre, here, if that would help.'

'Thank you, sir. I'm sorry to have troubled you.'

'Any time, Doctor. Whenever you're—er—worried.'

In the exchange of a smile she left him.

The afternoon passed quickly and was filled with interest. When Jane had seen her own patients (fortunately there was no one else very troublesome) she was asked to sit in with Dr Graves and pick up what practical knowledge she could.

While they were sharing tea and sandwiches at half-past four he said suddenly:

'Question time is now. What do you want to know, Jane?'

She was surprised and pleased that he addressed her in this off-duty manner, though there was no one else present at the time. He hadn't been so relaxed since she had been invited to dinner.

'Disseminated sclerosis, sir,' she mused. 'Does it always progress?'

'We haven't found a way to stop it yet,' he sighed. 'But it's usually so slow that this man Hetherington, who is now fifty-nine, may well live to be an octogenarian, though not a very active one. He will gradually complain of pains in the back, develop an awkward gait and become mentally sluggish. Drugs and sedatives can help a lot, of course, but they don't cure.'

'I must read it up,' Jane decided.

'My library is still at your disposal,' he told her. 'I don't hear that you spend much time up at the Retreat.'

She didn't like to tell him what Lyn Forrester thought of his housekeeper's reactions to visitors and yet sensed a reprimand in his tone.

'I haven't a car, you know, sir,' she told him.

'A bus passes the door exactly on the hour, every hour,' he dismissed this, 'and returns to Northingham at twenty-five to the hour.'

'I didn't know that,' she faltered.

'So how about coming up on Saturday?'

'I—I can't on Saturday, sir.'

'Please yourself,' he said coldly. 'I think we had better get on, don't you?'

She felt that he was disappointed in her; that he probably was concluding she didn't want to learn, whereas she couldn't read enough about anything connected with her chosen profession. She was rather sorry, now, that she had so glibly promised to baby-sit for the registrar at any time, when she was probably expected to spend her spare time more profitably.

'I'll do it this once, anyhow,' she decided, 'and then see how things go.'

During the week she thought a lot about Mr Hetherington and wondered at her preoccupation with one patient. Then, in the middle of one night when she was occupying the cubicle bed in Casualty which meant that she was 'on call' she suddenly knew the reason for it. The farmer had vaguely reminded her of someone else with similar symptoms, and that someone was Harry Esher, her mother's favourite escort and friend.

Of course! Harry was getting short tempered and aggressive because he was ill. He was finding it difficult to be the life and soul of any party, as he had once been. She remembered how he had knocked over the lamp and found difficulty in righting it again; how his hand had trembled and the way he had shoved it into his pocket as though its behaviour was an embarrassment to him.

Elaine mustn't marry him. She must be prevented at all costs from acquiring a husband who would—in time—become a helpless invalid. After her strong and splendid Ralph, Elaine wouldn't be able to stand such a thing.

There and then, in the middle of the night, she wanted to rush out to Hadrian's Retreat and tell Richard Graves all about Harry and her suspicions, but quickly realised this was impracticable. She must have patience and not allow herself to get so worried about people.

What good would she be now—shivering with dread—if somebody needed her in a hurry?

The very next moment she was called to the maternity ward where a young mother was haemorrhaging rather badly and found—to her relief—that her efficiency was apparently quite unimpaired.

On Saturday evening she went early to the address Dr Forrester had given her, being anxious to meet the twins before they went to bed.

They were lovely children, fair and blue eyed like their mother, though the girl, Carmel, was almost twice the size of her brother. He had decided to be petulant and complained of feeling sick, but Lyn assured the visitor that he made a habit of this whenever she wanted to go out.

'Why don't you ever stay home, Mummy?' the child

then demanded, finding his first gambit had failed to impress. 'We never have a play with *you*.'

'Because I have to go out to work, darling,' she said promptly. 'We haven't got a daddy, you see.'

'You're not working today.'

'No—well'—Lyn grimaced at Jane, who was thinking that if she had two such lovely children she would wish to be with them whenever possible and not hand them over to strangers—'Mummy still wants to go out sometimes.'

'Wiv Uncle Richard?'

'Yes. I must go and pretty myself up.'

Into the vacuum which followed her departure Jane sank on to the settee with the latest adventures of Rupert Bear, which she had thoughtfully purchased, leaving the twins to take their time in assessing her.

'Can you read?' Carmel asked gravely.

'Yes. I like a book to have pictures too, though. They're much jollier with pictures.'

'I can read pictures,' said Carmel. 'Shall we share it?'

'Certainly. What about you, Nigel?'

'I feel very sick,' he said stubbornly.

When Lyn came down the stairs, looking positively radiant, she gave Jane her instructions.

'The children are bathed promptly at seven and have a cup of cocoa and a biscuit to follow. You shouldn't have any trouble with them. You seem to be going down quite well for a beginner.'

'And if I did need you I could reach you at Dr Graves'?'

'Yes. But there shouldn't be any need for that. I'll be back before midnight.'

Jane found herself wishing she could be going off on a date with Richard Graves. She found herself drawn to him more and more with time's passing. How did Lyn see him? Had they got as far as being sweethearts? What was he like as a man—a lover?

'Do you think we could play Indians, now?' Nigel was asking. 'I'm not to run about so I'll be the Big Chief and have my tepee under the table. You two can be palefaces and I'll shoot you.'

'It's all right,' Carmel assured her fellow paleface. 'They're only rubber arrows. They don't really hurt.'

CHAPTER TEN

JANE put her two charges to bed, told them a story and discovered that they were both fast asleep long before she had finished. She had not found the children difficult at all, and far from being spoilt little Nigel merely appeared to desire a great deal of personal attention and affection, which no doubt Lyn found exhausting since she had to be the breadwinner as well.

But having one's own children must be absolutely wonderful, Jane decided, and sighed that there must be the necessary preliminary of finding oneself a suitable husband before one could indulge in such a pleasure.

Of course, she pondered, as she looked down on the sleeping babes, thinking she would never be able to tear herself away from the sight of their composed, angelic faces, having children of one's own was not a one evening's novelty. They had to be reared, fed, nursed and understood and they were always there, tomorrow and the next day until they were fledged into the world and able to take care of themselves.

Still, it must be a precious bondage and one any true woman would be proud to bear.

Jane went downstairs at last, realising that unless she took herself severely in hand she would be guilty of doting on someone else's offspring, something their own mother was probably far too sensible to do.

She made herself a cup of coffee and settled down to read in the sitting room, a very modern room with peculiarly-shaped chairs and geometrical patterns on both curtains and carpet. Lyn had very few medical books and an airy taste in fiction, but Jane settled down with the radio playing background music that soothed and became involved in 'Modern neuro-surgery' without any real enthusiasm.

Still, one could not be a qualified doctor and fail to respond to an expert's treatise on that part of the human body whose activities direct all the rest, and she was really interested when just after nine o'clock the front doorbell rang.

Jane sprang up as though shot. Was Lyn back already? But surely she would have a key. Then what about Lyn's mother? She was sure Mrs Keble was supposed to have gone to stay with friends for a couple of days. But surmising would not answer the door and if the bell kept on ringing it might disturb the children.

She flung open the door in the small hall and was just as amazed to see Richard Graves as he was to see her.

'Well—good evening!' he greeted her.

'Good evening, sir!'

'Aren't you going to ask me in?'

'Er—yes. Do please come in. Is Dr Forrester with you?'

'No. I've come to see the boy. If he's asleep we won't wake him.'

Jane felt suddenly very happy to see him for any reason whatsoever. At that moment she did not question this. It was something she would have to take up with herself later when she was alone.

'They're both asleep,' she told him. 'Would you like to go upstairs now or have some coffee? I've just made some.'

'Then we'll have coffee. I have had a most distracting evening so far. I have been at the Infirmary.'

'Oh.' She poured him coffee and watched him spoon

demerara sugar into it plentifully. He took lemon in his
tea, she had noticed, but apparently had a sweet tooth
for coffee.

'What a pity!' she sympathised. 'Dr Forrester will be
waiting for you at home.'

'She isn't,' he denied. 'I have just come from there. I
thought I had better come and see wee Nigel before I
settled down to a late dinner and a book. I see you're
reading Oundle.'

'Yes. Dr Forrester appears to have a leaning towards
the surgical side.'

'Her husband's, more likely. He had a surgical
appointment in Newcastle.'

Jane was slowly facing the realisation that Lyn
Forrester had lied to her. She had said she would be at
Hadrian's Retreat, but Richard Graves did not appear
to have been expecting her at all since he looked in no
way disappointed. If there had been any emergency she
wouldn't have known where to find the children's
mother, which was monstrous. She began to feel angry,
not only on her own behalf but on the consultant's. How
dare Lyn use his name so lightly, as though he was
expected to be with her whenever she decided to take an
evening off!

'What are *you* doing here, Jane?' asked Richard
Graves, suddenly.

'I'm baby-sitting. Doctor Forrester is glad to get out
sometimes.'

'Only sometimes?' joked he. 'Lyn's responsibilities
seem to be liberally shared by all she knows. However,
we can't all be so popular.' Was there bitterness in that
remark? Did he mind Lyn being popular?

'Is this why you couldn't come up to the Retreat this
evening?' he asked her soberly.

'Yes. I had already arranged to do it.'

'Don't be too liberal with your spare time,' he warned her, and then laughed. 'I had thought you would be seeking gayer places on some lad's arm when you were freed from the demands of our common area of operations?'

'No lad asked me,' she retorted as lightly.

He gave her a long, slow, appraising stare which was not that of a senior consultant for his most junior houseman.

'Laggard lad,' he decided, almost to himself, and jumped to his feet as she almost drowned in the tide of her blushes. 'Shall we look in on *gemini*?'

Now that the two hearts were beating slower, in the deeps of infant sleep, the boy was noticeably unnaturally pale, almost blue as though circulation had ceased.

'Is he going to be all right?' Jane asked in concern as her senior took the pulse and temperature of the small invalid without disturbing him in the lower of the bunk beds.

'You've not taken to worrying about *him*, have you?' he mocked her. 'My, but you have the outsize in compassion!'

'I was a normal, active child,' she retorted, somewhat stung. 'And I happen to think that at least is everyone's right.'

'So it is,' he sighed. 'There's no reason why young Nigel shouldn't be perfectly normal by the time he's seven. He'll probably have his operation during next year. You will be miles away, by then, worrying about someone else.'

'I wouldn't be a doctor if I wasn't what I am,' she went on. 'I hope I'll always be worried by the Mr Hetheringtons and the Nigels of this world.'

'You're too serious, Jane,' he told her softly, for a moment taking her fingers and squeezing them in his own. 'I enjoy teasing you. You have hackles. Did you know? When I see them rise it amuses me. You're a good little doctor, and a pleasant and companionable young woman. You mustn't blush so. I find it hard to believe that you have not had your share of such compliments.'

'Oh, dear!' thought poor Jane. 'I'm in danger of falling in love with this man who merely delights in teasing me and seeing me blush! How could I possibly have got into this state knowing how impossible the whole situation is? I'm not a teenager. I've been in love before. Or have I? Being in love with Kent never gave me this awful, hopeless ache where my heart should be. I must come to my senses—and quickly!'

Apparently in no hurry to leave, Richard Graves once more sat opposite her in the sitting room. On the stereo a recording of Rachmaninov's second piano concerto sounded a liquid background to their conversation.

'My brother used to play that,' he told her. 'Hopelessly. He has a wonderful appreciation of music but a poor interpretation. Whenever he hears anything as it should be played he rushes out to buy the music and then proceeds to murder it. I remember when we were boys and the Warsaw Concerto was the rage. He became so fed up with my jocund remarks that we had a fight which lasted a record twenty-four and a half rounds and exhausted us both. He was the elder but I was the taller and it was impossible to gain a decision. We both finally shouted "Pax" and fell down to recover at leisure.'

'You have always been a tease, then?' she asked shyly. 'Are you a big family, sir?'

'No. Only the two of us. Harry is in Harley Street. It was he who knew your father.'

'Sir Henry Graves?' Jane asked excitedly. 'Why didn't I connect you? He has often been to see us, especially when we lived in London. Who would have thought that I would one day be your houseman?'

'The world does get smaller with reminiscence, doesn't it, Jane? Let us to other things before we discover we're related.'

'Wouldn't you have liked to have a sister, sir?'

'Not like you.'

'And what's wrong with me?'

'I don't happen to regard you as sister material,' he said, leaning towards her. 'You may be everything that's admirable in a woman, Jane, but I refuse to have you for my sister. I must go and face Mrs Morrison, now, with the charred remains of my dinner. When shall I tell her you'll be coming?'

'You mean to do some reading, sir?'

'I mean exactly that.'

'And you're sure she wouldn't mind my coming?'

'Why on earth should my housekeeper mind my assistants doing as I advise them?' he asked in some surprise. 'It was she who told me you hadn't been near the place.'

'I will hope to come next Wednesday, when I finish early,' Jane said quickly. 'It's very kind of you to allow me the use of your library.'

He left a few moments later and Jane felt angry again with Lyn Forrester for having apparently lied on a second account. Was Lyn really all she pretended to be? Could one believe anything she said, hereafter, as the simple truth?

It was well after midnight before Dr Forrester returned home, and Jane—who had told the night porter at the gatehouse that she would be back by twelve thirty—was awaiting her ominously in the hall. She saw a brilliant red coupé roar off into the night before the door closed.

'Oh, dear! I *have* kept you late,' Lyn smiled disarmingly. 'You look awfully angry, Jane, and now you won't come and help me out ever again, will you?'

'That remains to be seen, of course,' the other said gruffly. 'By the way, Dr Graves called and looked at Nigel. I gave him coffee. I thought you would approve of that.'

'Oh, yes?' Lyn's smile became a little fixed. 'I couldn't meet him as arranged. I met someone quite by accident and we've been talking about old times. You know how time flies when one's interested?'

Her lipstick was smudged and she was flushed and evasive, as one is when one has been indulging in a kissing session.

'You've been an absolute dear,' she effused. 'But I'm dead, now, and must get into bed. I hoped you had no trouble?' she asked as an afterthought.

'None, thank you,' said Jane, thinking that whereas Lyn was not expected on duty tomorrow, she would be on the wards from morning until night.

Of course there were no buses at this time and Jane set off, bad-temperedly, to walk the two miles to the hospital. She didn't normally accept lifts from strangers, but when a kindly lorry driver opened the door of his cab she jumped in without more ado.

The night porter was understanding as he admitted her, for she told him quite frankly what she had been doing.

'Dr Forrester's a right one,' he smiled. 'Just what I would expect of her. A real little merry widow she is.'

'Whose is the red Triumph?' Jane asked, pointing to the coupé now lined up in the residents' car park. 'I haven't seen that before.'

'It's young Mr Oundle's,' the porter said proprietorially. 'His dad's coughed that up. What it is to have a liberal dad, eh? He got delivery yesterday. Been christening it proper tonight, he has, the rascal! No doubt had a bit of stuff in it down Haltwhistle way. He just got back a few minutes before you did.'

If there was innuendo in the porter's words Jane didn't notice it. She was walking towards her room down the hushed corridors and pondering that Colin Oundle obviously knew Lyn Forrester far better than she did. Lyn could apparently be picked up at an ogle and impressed with the peacock show of an expensive new car and dad's openhandedness in other ways.

Feeling rather sick, Jane wondered what were the 'old times' these two had needed to discuss together and at such length.

CHAPTER ELEVEN

OLGA's letter was sharp and to the point and struck home with the impact of truth.

> My dear Jane [she had written],
>   What on earth is the matter with you nowadays? I'm beginning to suspect that you are in love, you write so carefully and clinically as though to prove that you have no emotions involved anywhere except in your work. As I know you differently I want to hear *immediately* who he is and why you're not talking about it to me, of all people . . .

'Really, Olga is so absurd at times!' Jane weakly protested before continuing to read.

> . . . You have told me fully about your wards and the clinic at which you assist; I feel I know Granny Burton and her 'bleeding ulcer', as she so correctly calls it, quite intimately, as also I now know your Mr Hetherington and Miss Biggs as though they were my own patients. If you don't stop it I shall retaliate by telling you all about *my* problem cases; my prized AB negative and my young haemophiliac and the old dear whose veins collapse the moment one even shows her a hypodermic. But for this time I will spare you and speak of something which, though not more interesting, is at least more fascinating at times. I mean the *men*, my dear, and surely you have those at Northingham, too? Since your beloved Potts passed on to join

the happy unemployed in heaven; and hasn't it occurred to you that if there are no sick and no hospitals in the next world we are going to be rather at a loose end when we get there? You haven't mentioned your new chief much at all. He was good-looking, I remember, and had an acid wit which he used at your expense. Has he improved on closer acquaintance or has he died, too? . . .

'Really! Olga is so irreverent!' Jane protested silently, vaguely disturbed at being reminded of Richard Graves' existence.

. . . Who is taking you out, and would I approve of him? We have a new resident, name of Johnson, very good-looking and with those deep, dark eyes which play havoc with one's blood sugar. As he's in residence here he must be either single or separated from his wife. My life is meaningless until I know. You can't imagine how important the question is to me and yet he hasn't spoken to me yet only to say 'Will you see to the catheter charts today, Dr Wyatt?' and even that has me tingling to my toes. I suppose we women doctors are dreadfully repressed, but at least *I* have set my repressions down on paper. You didn't come home for your first long weekend, but how about your next, which must be about due as you have been at Northingham for three months now?

Longing to see you,
Love, Olga

Jane sighed as she folded the missive and put it away. Olga could get rid of her repressions so easily, and had always been able to discuss the most personal and intimate things with her friend, but Jane's role had always been that of listener and her own problems she had kept to herself. She couldn't tell anyone—not even Olga—that she had been foolish enough to fall in love, not with either a fellow houseman or a resident, but with the chief himself. Knowing the situation was hopeless made her even more secretive about the affair, and she was waiting with a dumb and aching patience for recovery, which must only be a matter of time, as all things were.

It startled her to be reminded that she had been three months at Northingham and that in another three months she would be moving on to the surgical side to gain experience under Mr France. It was at present awful to contemplate not seeing Richard (as she privately thought of him) during the bi-weekly rounds or at the clinic. Also she had been attending his house to read during her spare evenings, and occasionally he dropped into the library and made some point clearer to her or took his coffee with her and chatted about medicine in general, not realising how she hung on every word, not only because it was wise but because the voice thrilled and excited her as a woman.

After the change-over she could not, in all fairness, still go to Hadrian's Retreat on the same footing. As Mr France's houseman she would be expected to at least show some interest in the surgical side and read up the subject when she was off duty. No matter where her heart or her true interests lay a practising doctor was required to have a general experience to meet all emergencies.

Another damper on her secret passion was Lyn Forrester, who made no secret of the fact that one day she expected to be Mrs Graves.

'Richard and I would be married tomorrow if it wasn't for the fact that I want to gain more experience in my job,' she once told Jane. 'I made the mistake of marrying in haste, once, and I shan't do it again. Richard is very patient, bless him, and the children adore him, but I shall wait at least another year before committing myself.'

'But you're engaged, of course?' Jane inquired, not so much out of curiosity as incredulous that anyone could have the chance of marrying Richard Graves and not taking it promptly.

'No. We're not even engaged,' Lyn said brightly. 'Technically we're both quite free, but our understanding goes beyond baubles such as rings.'

Jane had quickly overcome her irritation with Dr Forrester and her apparent disregard for the strict truth. Although she had vowed not to sit with the children again to be treated so inconsiderately for her pains, she had relented when Lyn passed on little messages purporting to come from the twins.

'Nigel says will the nice lady come and read him some more Rupert soon?'

'Carmel wants to know when you'll be playing dressing up with her again. She says you let her wear real nylons.'

'I laddered mine,' Jane explained with a smile, 'but I had a spare pair in my bag. I gave Carmel the damaged ones and she entertained herself for fully an hour hobbling about in those and my shoes. That gave Nigel and me plenty of time for Rupert.'

So Jane had allowed Lyn to impose on her several more times. Whom she went out with on these occasions she didn't say, but as she wasn't actually engaged to Richard Graves it was nobody's business but her own. Jane was not going to appoint herself moralist as well as baby-sitter, but though she went in high hopes to Lyn's house on those Saturday evenings, Dr Graves never again turned up unexpectedly to keep her company.

It was now late March and an early spring had coaxed out the first of the daffodils and was tempting the apple blossom to peep before its true time. The gardeners were busy in the grounds of Northingham Infirmary, hoeing and pruning and giving the lawns their first mowing of the season.

Jane was strolling under the aspens, after a late lunch, when Dr Forrester approached her.

'Jane, you simply have to sit for me on the evening of the eighteenth of next month. I know you're free. I've looked at the roster. Mother's away for that weekend and I simply can't get anyone else.'

'All right,' Jane agreed. 'If it's an important date for you, of course I'll oblige.'

'It's the Founder's Day dance. Actually you'll be invited, too. Will you mind?'

Jane hesitated only for a moment.

'I won't be expected to attend, will I?'

'There's no compulsion, my dear. Actually these official do's are rather a bore, but *I* won't be bored.' She winked and laughed knowingly.

'All right, then,' agreed generous Jane. 'You can count on me.'

When she saw the invitation to the dance lying on the linoleum of her room floor she was somewhat regretful. She liked to dance, like all young things, and now knew her young colleagues sufficiently well for them to spoil and tease her a little.

'Remember I shall require you for a rather dashing tango I specialise in,' said Reg McArdle, the surgical houseman, who would be taking Jane's place later in the year. 'I do a real Valentino.'

'Well, do it with somebody else, Reg. I'm not going.'

'Not going to the Founder's Day do?' he asked incredulously. 'All the consultants and Committee members will be there. They actually unbend and become human until they all turn back into pumpkins again at midnight. You can't not go to this affair, Jane, my girl.'

'I hear it's not compulsory, so I'm not going. Actually I have another date.'

'My boss told me I had better be there,' Reg went on. 'All the sisters are invited and I'll have to do my share of dancing with them. There are one or two under thirty, but on the whole it must be the high spot of the hospital year for most of the old dears.'

'I don't think I will be required to dance with the sisters,' Jane twinkled.

'No, but you might have made it tolerable for *me*,' Reg said darkly.

'Honestly, Jane,' interposed Phil Wade, who was doing six months on obstetrics and gynae, 'you should really show up at these do's, irrespective of personal preference. Half of us will be bored to tears, but we can't cock a snook at the old Founder, whoever that dear soul might have been. Does anybody here know?'

While they were finding out Jane made her escape. She was somewhat startled at being confronted by Richard Graves a few days later. There was a coldness in his eyes for which she couldn't at first account.

'I have heard a rumour that you are not attending the Founder's Day dinner and dance, Dr Pilgrim.'

'That's right, sir. I heard attendance was not compulsory.'

'Naturally. This isn't the army. But some things are expected of one without being compulsory.'

Jane said nothing.

'Perhaps you will agree to working on call and so release somebody who would like to attend?'

'I'm sorry. I can't do that, sir.'

The voice became positively icy.

'Then you have other plans for the evening?'

'That's right, sir.'

It would have been the simplest matter in the world to explain that she was baby-sitting for Dr Forrester to release her, but somehow she thought this might cause discord between the lovers. He might make things difficult for Marilyn, calling it taking advantage of the firm's junior, and she already knew how scorching his very disapproval could be. So she stood her ground determining that where she was not compelled to go she refused to be driven by any darkling looks directed upon her.

'Then I hope you have a very enjoyable evening away from us,' he said bluntly, 'seeing that you apparently find no enjoyment in the prospect of saluting those who made our hospital a fact. The young are inclined to forget that sacrifices might once have been made on their behalf. Good afternoon, Doctor.'

Jane smarted under this for the rest of the day, and finally bared her heart to Dr Forrester as they put up a drip together in the men's ward.

'He was absolutely unbearable,' she said at last, 'as though my first duty was to attend this function. I hope I'm not the only one to be missing.'

'Of course you won't be,' Lyn said promptly. 'I went last year, as Richard's guest, and they were mainly old fuddy-duddies. All the housemen had made excuses at the last minute. I'll say something to make it all right with Richard on your behalf. Leave it to me. Of course if you think he would rather have you than me—?'

Jane smiled at this obvious absurdity and the subject was tacitly dropped.

CHAPTER TWELVE

STRANGELY enough Jane felt rather out of things by tea-time on the day of the Founder's dinner and dance, an event which was to be held in Northingham's Town Hall and attended by the Mayor and Corporation.

Apparently the other housemen were not intending to drop out at the last minute; they were busily pressing their dinner jackets or flattering some homely minded nurse or domestic to do so for them. As they were allowed to take a guest they were also busily assessing one another's conquests in this regard and there was much goodnatured leg pulling in the junior common room as they were served with tea, scones and cakes by the maid on duty.

'That was a sneaky thing to do,' Phil Wade accused Colin Oundle. 'Asking Daphne behind all our backs. Being the hospital Chairman's daughter I suppose you're just taking her to do yourself some good, eh?'

'And using that red bomb of his to impress, of course,' added Reg McArdle. 'I thought you liked older women, anyway, Colin? I've heard rumours that you might be taking on a family.'

'Sour grapes,' retorted Colin, ignoring the latter innuendo. 'You all wanted Daphne but she decided you were a bit on the juvenile side. You have no finesse, gentlemen, and it sticks out like a cauliflower ear. Anyway, who's brave enough to go with you, Reg?'

'I'm taking that smashing little redhead from maternity. I should imagine I'll have a better time than you.

Daphne Cato is a bit on the cool side, convent educated and all that.'

'And you're not going, Jane?' Phil Wade asked regretfully. 'I'm sorry. We're fated never to see you off duty, it seems. Who is he?'

'Who is who?'

'This bloke of yours who won't come to the do with you. I suppose he doesn't dance or something stuffy like that.'

'I have no idea what you're talking about.'

'Neither have I, actually. I was fishing.'

'Well, there's no "he" involved, except for one delightful four-year-old. I'm baby-sitting this evening.'

'Good lord! The maternal instinct. I didn't realise women doctors had it. Anyway, I'm really sorry you can't come along this evening.'

'Thanks. But I'm sure that by all I hear you won't have time to miss me. Tell me all about it tomorrow.'

So she was the odd one out, as she had feared, and although Dr Forrester had promised to speak on her behalf to Richard Graves, he had remained cool—though polite—with her ever since their last contretemps.

She was off duty fairly promptly, and dressed simply for her intention of keeping two small children entertained and then bathing and putting them to bed. She glanced obliquely at the white and gold dress she would have worn if she had been going to the dance. It would have been nice to relax among those of her calling, for once . . .

Into a soft bag she packed a pair of old tights and a miniature nurse's uniform, for Carmel, and an ancient stethoscope for Nigel. They would be delighted to play 'doctors', she knew, and drag out all their dolls and soft toys to provide the necessary patients.

By now Jane had her own car, an ancient Wolseley which was heavy on petrol but had been carefully maintained by its previous owner. There were years of driving in the vehicle and she had affectionately dubbed it 'The Cardinal'.

It was much more convenient not having to rely on either buses or friends for one's transport, and there were shrieks of delight from the twins as the Wolseley was parked in a small cul-de-sac nearby and they saw Jane approaching.

'Darlings!' she greeted them as she admitted herself to the house. Mummy was in the bath, they told her, and making herself very pretty for the dance. Why wasn't she, Jane, going?

'Because Mummy and I can't both go. Anyway, I wanted to play with you.'

The hospital impedimenta were duly rejoiced over and tried out. Teddy, so Nigel said gravely, was very tired because something was wrong with his heart. He would have to have an operation to make him like other teddy bears.

Jane's own heart contracted as she realised how this four-year-old child always carried his infirmity with him, even in his play.

'If he was mine I would want to be comforting and loving him all the while,' she told herself, but also decided that this would probably be bad for the boy. Lyn's attitude of casual motherhood to fit in with the rest of her activities was probably far more practical in the long run.

The children were allowed to stay up to see their mother finally dressed, and Jane had to admit she was quite breathtaking.

She looked eminently sophisticated in a black sheath dress; black always complementing the naturally blonde.

Her fair hair was as short and shining as a cap.

She smiled, as Jane admired the effect. 'I suppose you people had better be off upstairs, now. We don't want you getting too excited.'

'Oh, Mummy, we were having such a good time with Aunty Jane—'

'She *isn't* your aunt,' Lyn said rather sharply to Carmel, then smiled to take the sting out of her words. 'I have a thing about adopted relationships. I don't know about you—'

'I don't mind one way or the other,' Jane admitted. 'Come along, children, and we'll have a boat race in the bath.'

Lyn looked thoughtfully after the little procession now eagerly wending its way up the stairs.

'I do not like thee, Doctor Fell-cum-Pilgrim,' she mused as she lit a cigarette. 'You are altogether too damned popular with other people, including *my* children. I'm not a sharer, I never was, and I think the sooner you get out of my life the better for all of us. Trying to be nice to you, when I want to bite you, is becoming a little too much of a strain.'

So Jane was busily occupied when she heard Lyn Forrester greet someone in the hall and soon afterwards leave the house. She tried to imagine Richard dressed up for the evening; he must look very distinguished and handsomer than ever in formal clothes.

She wished she could see them all in party mood, and especially Richard. Did he dance well? she wondered. With such a little time to spend on his 'firm' she would probably never know the answer to that now.

The twins were more excited and wakeful than usual and she read until her throat was hoarse before they finally dropped off in the middle of a sentence within seconds of each other. She pressed a light kiss upon each infant brow, in lieu of their mother, and crept downstairs feeling strangely depressed.

'Oh, dear!' she told herself sternly. 'Stop feeling like Cinderella and make yourself a cup of coffee.'

She also decided to answer Olga's letter if she could do so without committing herself. She gave a clever word picture of every male in the hospital, barring one.

'So there they all are,' she wrote playfully, 'and you'll be sorry to hear I'm not involved with any of them. The housemen are inclined to treat me like their sister, which is a relationship I enjoy, not having any brothers of my own. The residents are mostly married and if I write about my work and the patients it's because my life, at present, *is* all work and patients.' She then told Olga about her baby-sitting activities and described the twins. 'You ask about Richard Graves. He is still my chief and I don't think there's much else to tell . . .'

As the doorbell shrilled she automatically hushed it with her fingers to her lips, but there was no outcry from upstairs so she presumed the twins were now in deep slumber.

At first she thought Dr Forrester had returned unexpectedly when she opened the door and saw the fair haired woman shaking the rain from a plastic hood. The shower had been heavy, apparently, but was now over leaving the laurels in the small area of garden darkly shining.

'I'm Lyn's sister,' the newcomer introduced herself briefly, coming into the hall where she divested herself of a mac. 'I wouldn't have come troubling you but I've missed my train back to Newcastle. I shall stay the night.'

'Oh,' said Jane, somewhat at a loss. 'Would you like some coffee? I—I didn't know Dr Forrester had a sister.'

'She has two. I'm the younger one. Possibly that's

why,' she added ambiguously. 'Lyn's always afraid her family will be indiscreet in some way. Indiscretion,' she added darkly, 'being our middle name.'

Jane poured the newcomer some coffee, knowing that she was being covertly studied.

'You're quite pretty, really,' the woman said after a few minutes, 'and you don't want to spend your time bathing other people's children. That's no way to get some of your own, if you're so fond of them.'

'I don't think I'm ridiculous over children,' Jane justified herself. 'I don't stop and look in every pram like some women do. Dr Forester wanted to go to the Founder's Day dinner and asked me to baby-sit. She couldn't get anyone else.'

The other laughed shrilly as though at some private joke.

'That's rich. What's wrong with *me*? Or our mother? Lyn told mother to take the day off and that dear soul is at this very moment in Carlisle baby-sitting for Gwen, our elder sister. I'm a solicitor but I'm always available whenever Lyn needs me, not having to work those hopeless hours you doctors do. Anyway I'm here now. Is there anything else you would rather be doing?'

Trying to keep her anger in check Jane said clearly: 'I don't mind doing someone a favour, but your sister made it quite clear that if I went to the dinner she could not. She is my professional senior and I felt I must defer to her. After this, of course . . .'

The other woman laughed again.

'Don't take it too much to heart, dear. Lyn has learned to live by her wits and for some reason she doesn't want you to attend this affair. I should rush off and dress up and surprise her. The children will be in good hands. Don't worry about a thing.'

Jane's fury consumed her as she drove back to the

hospital. How dared Lyn Forrester keep her away from a hospital function by a mean trick? Why should she find anything objectionable in a junior houseman being seen relaxing in public? Only Lyn could answer to her own behaviour, but it was a case of twice bitten and never again as far as Jane Pilgrim was concerned.

She knew she would be too late for the dinner but still she couldn't resist making an appearance at the Town Hall if only to wrap Dr Forrester in the web of her own deceit. Anger had put roses into her cheeks and a flash in her eyes and she looked really lovely as she handed her coat to a flunkey at the Town Hall and was shown into a Palm Lounge where groups of people were drinking port and conversing while a band tuned up in the ballroom beyond.

'You came after all, Jane!' Phil Wade greeted her gladly, procuring a wineglass for her and admiring her appearance with his sand coloured eyes. 'Care for—?'

'I just want a word with Dr Forrester,' Jane said hastily, spotting Lyn standing near the Mayoral party but not of it. The Registrar's eyes opened wide in disbelief as Jane advanced, not a few masculine eyes following her determined progress.

Lyn was suddenly just as determined to escape and barged into the Mayoress's broad bosom, murmured apologies and then dodged round a pillar. She could go no further, for Richard Graves was advancing from the opposite direction. He looked amazed and delighted as Jane joined them.

'My dear Dr Pilgrim,' he greeted jovially. 'How nice to think you have decided a few hours' dalliance at our Vanity Fair will do you no harm. Lyn'—he turned to the Registrar—'I have bad news for you. You're wanted at the hospital to decipher your notes regarding Mrs Dee's medication. You might look in at the PP wing, too, to make sure all's well there.'

Dr Forrester turned away with a very bad grace, indeed, only to find Jane, like Nemesis, at her elbow.

'You needn't worry about your children,' that young lady said coldly. 'Your sister is staying the night. She says she is always available to baby-sit for you when you need her.'

Lyn, who hadn't had time to think of a suitable explanation for the inexplicable, turned on her heel and went without a word in the direction of the ladies' cloakroom.

Jane, feeling somewhat deflated as her anger evaporated quickly, found Richard Graves once more at her side and beckoning the wine waiter.

'To this must we drink,' he decided. 'Jane looking ravishing. You are, you know. I am being quite sincere.'

And looking up into the clear grey eyes she realised, with a sense of shock, that he really meant the compliment.

CHAPTER THIRTEEN

JANE was surprised to find that Richard Graves was still with her; that, all in a glance, he had taken in her appearance and thoroughly approved it, if one could judge by the somewhat proprietorial air with which he regarded her.

The band struck up the opening waltz and as Phil Wade somewhat hesitantly approached, Dr Graves said firmly: 'If you are thinking of asking Dr Pilgrim for the pleasure, young man, she happens to be so favouring me.'

As Phil coughed and slipped away, he said in an inquiring tone: 'Aren't you, Jane?'

She replied breathlessly: 'I shall be happy to dance with you,' and felt herself held firmly against him and swung expertly into the rhythm of the waltz.

For the first few seconds she was shy and a little unsure of herself, then she relaxed and felt his supporting arm squeeze her a little more tightly, as though he understood her feelings and was reassuring her in some way.

'I'm glad you decided to drop in,' he told her at length. 'You dance well.'

'Any woman is only a reflection of her partner,' Jane returned the compliment, and then noticed that his eyes remained smilingly upon hers.

'I'm sure that was not intended to be ambiguous,' he told her. 'But I wonder if your statement applies to other fields than the ballroom?'

Jane laughed to match his mood.

'I'm sure it does,' she assured him. 'You mean husbands and wives, of course?'

'And medical colleagues . . . ?'

'That should put me on my mettle. I have an idea you would wish the reflection to be brilliant in that particular field.'

He looked at her again and the smile died on her lips; but only because for a moment something dark and intense and new was in his gaze. The next second he was his own urbane self once more, and as the dance ended he suggested they take some refreshment together and led her to a small table behind a fragrant bank of flowers which provided a modicum of privacy from the eyes of the dancers.

'Am I monopolising you, Jane?' he then asked her seriously after signalling to a waiter. 'Do you mind? I see so little of you, really, apart from work.'

Did he, then, want to see more of her outside of working hours? she wondered.

'There isn't much left outside of work, sir,' she told him somewhat wryly. 'And I hope that *I'm* not monopolising *you*. You must know everybody here.'

'All apart from you,' he returned. 'And I would naturally like to know you a little better. This seems like a heaven-sent opportunity. You are always either ducking out, or turning every corner ahead of me; metaphorically speaking, of course.'

She stared at him, wondering why he appeared to mind not seeing much of her, and suddenly her heart gave a wild leap. If Lyn lied about one thing she certainly wouldn't hesitate to lie about another where her own interests were concerned. There was only her word for it that Richard Graves was romantically interested in her; that an engagement and marriage were pending upon her own whim. This might only be wishful thinking on her part and not a fact at all, which was why she had gone to such trouble to remove competition from her path and cause stupid misunderstandings between Jane and her mentor. If this man across from her was encouraging her to step over the invisible line which separated professional colleagues of differing status, but not a man from a woman, then she would not hesitate in answering his invitation. Should their better acquaintance only last this one evening she would make the best of it and have something, at least, to remember.

Therefore, after enjoying a drink during which they solemnly saluted the future, he again asked her to dance, and they danced almost every dance together; the exception being a Valeta where he dutifully partnered Matron and Jane found herself claimed by the Mayor, a portly gentleman who joked that he carried his 'corporation' around with him.

After that, all too soon, it was the last waltz, and Jane felt that she must be in some heavenly dream as a masculine cheek quite deliberately pressed for a moment against her own. She leaned back to smile at him, then the music slowed and he whirled her into the shadow of a group of potted palms.

All in a moment he had seized his opportunity and kissed her parted lips with the swiftness of an arrow.

'Richard!' she said aloud, mouthing his name for the first time. 'Oh!' She put her hand to her lips. 'I'm sorry.'

'For what?' he asked whimsically. 'Surely it is I who have offended, if anyone.'

'No, I'm not offended,' she told him from afar off.

He took both her hands. 'Then perhaps I am offending someone else who has a better right?' he inquired.

'No one else has any right.'

'Say that again adding "Richard".'

'No one else has any right to kiss me, Richard.'

'Good! Then—'

From close at hand came another voice, Marilyn Forrester's.

'Why are you hiding behind a palm tree with a houseman, Richard? Really! Be your age. Everybody's talking about you.'

Suddenly the whole wonderful evening exploded into absurdity. Of course she was only a junior houseman and of course he was a consultant physician and so far above her professionally as to make his attentions appear ridiculous.

Jane turned away, angry and humiliated yet once again, and so she didn't hear what went on in conversation between her two superiors.

'Actually I *was* being my age for once, Lyn, and enjoying myself. I'm not an old fogey on pension, and I'm sure if everybody's talking about me, as you say, they're being more generous than you in their conclusions.'

She flushed angrily.

'You know how easily these young people get ideas into their befuddled little heads. She'll be expecting you to do the right thing by her next.'

'How interesting!' he said. 'A woman's mind is always a revelation to me. It apparently occupies such a small area.'

'There's no need to be rude.'

'I'm sorry. Rudeness shall be your prerogative.'

'Nor do I wish to quarrel with you, Richard.' Lyn's eyes flashed dangerously.

'Then the way to achieve that is surely not to interfere with me when I am perfectly able to conduct my own affairs.'

'Go on, then! Make a fool of yourself.'

'Thank you. I'm sure it's long overdue.' He bowed to her mockingly, leaving her seething, as he saw Jane emerge from the ladies' cloakroom wearing a coat over her attractive dress.

Her glance was cooler now, veiled against him.

'May I see you home, Jane?'

'No, thanks. I have my own car.'

'Then have dinner with me some evening.'

'I haven't a night off for ages. I'm going home on my next long weekend.'

'Look here, I *have* to see you.'

'Why?' she asked him directly. 'This evening was fun but I don't expect anything more of it, you know. I can very easily forget everything, so please don't worry about it. I'm not the clinging sentimental type. Good-night, sir, and thank you for a lovely evening.'

He did not attempt to detain her and once again Lyn was at his elbow.

'The brush-off?' she inquired mock-sympathetically. 'The girl has more sense than I thought. She probably has a nice young man tucked away somewhere who is more her age.'

'She said not—' he said sharply, and then realised he could easily give himself away in anger. 'I hope she has.' He tried to sound enthusiastic. 'Nice young men and women belong together.'

'Am I forgiven?' Lyn wheedled, sliding her arm through his.

He surveyed her as though she was a stranger suddenly. He had known her husband, had thought he knew her, but this acid-tongued, mean-minded shrew he didn't know at all. She had driven Jane away from him as though she had a right to be jealous of his friendships, and he had never—even remotely—allowed her this right at all. He was suspicious of her; could very easily actively dislike her; therefore he was careful how he spoke.

'There's really nothing to forgive,' he said quietly.

'Good. I thought you were mad at me and I would really lose sleep over that. We're such old friends. I rely on you, Richard. Johnny always told me I could do that. Little Pilgrims come and go but *I* go on for ever. You haven't even told me whether I look nice or not.'

She posed blatantly, her dress rather too revealing for perfect taste, but she had a very good figure.

'You look very nice, Lyn.'

'Right. Are you taking me home or have I to throw myself on somebody else's good nature?'

'I'll take you home, of course.'

In the cloakroom her eyes became dark with anger. He was proving to be hard work, his politeness a cover for his private thoughts from which she now felt herself to be excluded. It was a damned shame she had been recalled to the hospital and so left a clear field for that Pilgrim brat to make her impact. Pilgrim had only done it out of pique because she was mad at her, Lyn. There would probably be another showdown in the morning, but she wasn't going to take a lot of cheek from a junior houseman, no matter how much she might be made to appear in the wrong.

Jane found sleep elusive. Whenever she closed her eyes she was once again dancing and feeling that closely shaven cheek disconcertingly near her own. Why had he kissed her? It was only for devilment, of course, but it had meant much more than that to her and she was ashamed to remember how she had given herself away with that sudden, eruptive 'Richard!'

Now he would know that she thought of him by his name privately, and he would be amused and intrigued to know why.

If she thought he was serious . . . ! But she couldn't really believe in his seriousness. It was terrible to become involved with one's professional senior and then be let down in the end.

She was tired and alarmed and afraid.

At three o'clock in the morning she crept down to the kitchen at the end of the residents' corridor and made herself a cup of cocoa. As she sat drinking the soothing liquid on the side of her bed she sought the thoughts which would let her mind find the peace which would allow her body to sleep.

It was really very simple, she discovered eventually. No matter what might happen she mustn't repulse Richard again. He might be playing with her, but she would have to find out. It was the dread of there being nothing more between them which was keeping her awake.

On the morrow she would find some way of letting him know that she would like to see him privately if it could be arranged.

Once she had promised herself this she was soon fast asleep.

During the round on Monday morning Jane found she had no opportunity of speaking to the chief without Dr Forrester being present. He did not even look in her direction, that she was aware of, though she was not to know that he was resisting doing anything likely to stimulate Lyn's spiteful interest once again.

Jane had decided to say nothing more to Lyn Forrester on the subject of her deception. She thought it was enough that the registrar should know that she had been exposed for the cheat she was, but Lyn did not look unduly perturbed on their next meeting, and after a few hours she was apparently as blithe as ever, trying to draw her junior into conversation and not in the least put out when Jane refused to be drawn.

When Richard Graves had gone to take coffee in the senior common room, after rounds, Jane—in desperation—wrote a little note and popped it into the pigeonhole under his name in the main staff corridor while on her way to the dispensary.

She had memorised every word she had written.

Dear Dr Graves,

Thank you for your kind invitation for me to have dinner with you in the near future. I was very tired after the dancing and hope you did not think me too abrupt at the time. Actually I would like to accept your invitation but I am on call most evenings this week in view of my forthcoming long weekend off duty.

I hope you will accept my explanation, and perhaps you can suggest an alternative plan for our meeting again.

Yours very sincerely . . .

Jane handed the ward-list in at the dispensary window and panicked as she pondered that Richard might consider her note to be colossal cheek. She would take it out of the rack on her way back to the ward and nobody would be any the wiser.

The square blue envelope had disappeared, however, along with his other mail. He would have read it by now and perhaps was laughing to think that she had taken him so seriously.

She then noticed a bent, blue square in her own pigeonhole and recognised her own writing on the envelope with a line drawn through it and her name superimposed.

Her heart thudded as she drew from the envelope a thin sheet of paper torn from a diary.

'I will be lunching at the Border Arms,' was written without preamble. 'Meet me there at one-fifteen.'

The note was not even signed but it made Jane so happy that she pressed it to her lips before putting it in her pocket and almost dancing back to the ward.

Her heart felt lighter than for a long time as the rest of the morning sped by. She loved her work and she loved her chief, and as her work was also his work she felt twice as happy performing it.

CHAPTER FOURTEEN

At one o'clock Lyn Forrester's head appeared round Sister Godolphin's office door. Jane was within hastily writing up a new admission's chart before leaving for her luncheon appointment.

'Oh, Dr Pilgrim, I've caught you in time.'

Jane's heart sank inexplicably.

'Yes, Dr Forrester?'

'Mr Witton is having another rigor so I have given instructions for the transfusion to be stopped until Dr Graves sees him again. Perhaps you wouldn't mind watching him until he has settled down?'

'I was lunching out, actually,' Jane said rather dully.

'Oh! Well, that's too bad. It's all in the game, though, isn't it? After all, *I* had to leave in the middle of the dance the other evening when duty called.'

'Yes, of course,' Jane said quickly. 'It's all in the game, as you say, Dr Forrester. It's fatal to make any arrangements.'

'I had better dash before mine are messed up,' Lyn said with a smiling shrug. 'If you want me I'll be at the Border Arms,' she added.

Jane's eyebrows shot up in surprise.

'Is anything wrong, Dr Pilgrim?'

'Why, no. Nothing at all, Dr Forrester.'

'I thought for a moment you resented *my* going out to lunch when you are unable to. I'm having lunch with my favourite boy-friend come hell or high water. Anyway, cheer up! *You'll* be a registrar one day and able to shove your housemen around.'

When she had assured herself that Mr Witton was comfortable, with a temperature now nearing normal thanks to hot drinks and extra blankets, Jane felt in her pocket for Richard's note, but it was no longer there.

She carefully shook out her handkerchief and the other contents of the pocket without success.

It served her right, she told herself severely, for so sentimentally hanging on to an unsentimental suggestion that she take her luncheon as one of a threesome

'I see enough of Lyn Forrester here,' she decided somewhat savagely. 'Probably it would have developed into a staff-meeting, or something.'

She 'phoned the hotel as soon as she could but was told that Dr Graves had just left.

'I suppose Lyn told him how *I* was occupied,' she decided philosophically as she trailed along to the staff dining room to partake of what must, at this time, be termed the remains of a hospital lunch.

In the bar of the Border Arms Lyn Forrester raised the gin and tonic her companion had ordered for her and watched Richard Graves stalk somewhat offendedly from the dining room out into the street.

'That'll teach him to make dates with housemen!' she said savagely, and crumpled a small piece of paper into a pill before shying it in the direction of a waste basket.

'Whatever are you talking about?' asked Colin Oundle.

'I often talk to myself, darling, or hadn't you noticed?'

'I had noticed. But what was that crack about housemen? Isn't a houseman's hospitality as good as that of your more eminent friends?'

'Are you drunk, darling? You always get nasty when you've had more than enough. Now buy me another before I make up my mind never to see you again.'

'Make that a promise,' Colin said clearly, 'and I'll buy you a whole bottle, sweetie.'

Jane found herself travelling south towards King's Cross without having enjoyed a personal chat with Richard Graves after all. She had formally apologised for the broken luncheon appointment only to be told: 'That could not be helped. I quite understand,' and the invitation was not, to her disappointment, repeated.

She was not to know that Lyn Forrester, having discovered the note on the Ward Office floor and burned with resentment over it, had deliberately put herself alongside Richard in the bar of the Border Arms for an apéritif, eyeing his mounting impatience with malicious satisfaction.

Finally he asked her: 'Have you seen Dr Pilgrim, by any chance?'

'I'm always seeing her, darling. She's continually under my feet. Why?'

'Oh, I just wondered what she was doing.'

'Seeing to old Witton's rigor, I shouldn't wonder. She mentioned that she had a luncheon appointment but assured me it wasn't important. Otherwise I would have relieved her, of course.'

Thus, Richard, having been dismissed as 'unimportant', had sourly taken his luncheon alone and been less than friendly when he and the houseman had met over Mr Witton's bed some time later.

He told himself that he was having none of this blow hot blow cold business. He was attracted to this golden brown pixie of a girl as he had never been attracted previously by any other female, but he was shy and emotionally self conscious, easily affronted and hurt, possibly because he had left it rather later than most men to fall in love deeply for the first time.

He was well aware that Lyn coveted him for a role he did not relish. She wanted him to father her children with herself thrown in as an inducement. She had made this all quite clear by innuendo and for a short time he had been tempted. That had been before he discovered that Lyn was a Jekyll and Hyde sort of person and that her hidden self was meaner and less honest than he was prepared to tolerate in the woman who would bear his name. He was relieved that he had never actually declared himself and that she apparently had many men friends and was prepared to ration out her charms.

Jane he had endowed with virtues he now doubted she really possessed. He had thought her an earnest little pilgrim struggling up the hill of difficulty (her medical career) without a frivolous or insincere thought in her pretty little head. That she could write and invite his attentions and then casually shrug it all off as unimportant savoured of the coquette, however, and he naturally wondered if he had been mistaken in any other particular.

Jane went straight through to her mother's home in Surrey, wanting only to spend the next twenty-four hours in bed, relishing the fact that she would not be disturbed during that time. Elaine, however, wanted to talk, which was quite natural.

'Well, dear, how's it all going?'

'Oh, very well, Mother. I feel much more like a doctor, now, than I did when I qualified.'

'Are the—er—patients clean? I mean do they have vermin, things like that?'

Jane felt the familiar irritation which was like an allergy whenever she and her parent attempted to communicate.

'Mother, they're all as clean as you are. Northingham's a clean place with fresher country air than you get here. I like both the place and the people. They're really friendly.'

'I've heard about their friendliness, as you call it. In and out of one another's houses, which I would loathe. When they come to live in the South they're always writing to the papers that we're not continually popping in to see them and admire their horrid little children, therefore we are unfriendly.'

'Mother,' Jane said patiently. 'Please don't let us argue the merits of North and South this evening. I'm tired. How's Harry?'

'Why are you so continually concerned over Harry? Your letters have been quite peculiar. You tell me about some patient of yours called Hetherington and then ask after Harry; if he has seen a specialist yet. You don't think Harry and Hetherington are similarly afflicted, do you?'

'I don't know, Mother. I hope not.'

'As a matter of fact Harry has seen a specialist. He didn't feel well at all.'

'And—?' Jane prompted.

'There are to be more tests yet, but it does look as though something's seriously wrong with poor Harry.'

'Oh, Mother, I'm so sorry. I didn't want to be right, honestly. Who will look after him if the worst comes to the worst'

'*I* will, of course.'

'Mother! You can't. There are very good nursing homes and Harry isn't a poor man. He can afford to be properly cared for.'

'Your father always said'—Elaine grimly proclaimed—'that a third rate home was better than a first class hospital from any patient's point of view. I'm very fond of Harry. I shall marry him and I shall care for him. There's nothing *you* can do about it.'

'Oh, Mother, if it does turn out to be disseminated sclerosis it will break your heart to see him. Harry's a fine man. I can't say that he's *my* type but he's not the sort who will tolerate the degeneracy of his own body without impatience and ill-humour. Then when—and if—his mind becomes impaired *you* may lose patience with him. It's a long, chronic, ineluctable progression of symptoms that can only go from bad to worse. I won't let you saddle yourself with it. I *will* do something about it. I'll tell Harry not to allow you to sacrifice yourself for him.'

'Jane!' Elaine looked so angry she almost struck her daughter. Then she visibly relaxed and sighed. 'You will do no such thing,' she said quietly and determinedly. 'Having removed yourself from my orbit and gone your own way, you cannot descend on me at your convenience and interfere with me going mine. I know your age, of course, but I sometimes think you have had too little emotional experience and this makes you appear very young at times. When one loves one takes what is involved in loving without complaint. Of course one moans and groans at times but one doesn't try to walk through the corners. One doesn't plead, "Oh Lord, give me the loving without the pain." The one is begotten of the other. I loved your father and because of this I had to suffer his neglect. It's no use your rushing to his defence, my girl. Because he was your father and a clever doctor I had to be neglected or he wouldn't have been the man I loved. Don't you see that? I minded like hell but I wouldn't have gone back in time and not married him for all the tea in China. Now I love Harry in a different way. We're mature and we fancy the idea of growing old together. You won't put me off by telling me he's going to have to depend on me more and more as time goes on because of some progressive physical degeneracy. If you think that love can be bought off because it's scared of the consequences, my girl, you haven't the vaguest idea of what love is, and I sympathise with you on that account. You've been so busy learning the functions of the body you've neglected those of the heart.'

Jane's head was lowered and her cheeks were suddenly aflame. Elaine put her finger under her daughter's chin and regarded her quizzically.

'Or am I wrong about that?' she asked softly.

'Oh, Mother, I want to love someone like that,' she sighed swiftly. 'How does one ever get close enough?'

'One does, if one really means it.'

Jane withdrew from this new, unexpected intimacy and smiled.

'I am sorry I tried to intrude on your affairs, Mother,' she said wryly. 'You obviously know what you're about and for the very best reasons. I shall worry about you, of course. Allow me that.'

'I shall worry about myself quite often, but worry is a woman's constant shadow and it doesn't kill, as they say. A woman with nothing to worry her will eventually worry about the fact. It's much better knowing what you're worried about than wondering what it might be.'

'You're talking rubbish,' Jane accused. 'So it's time for bed. Do you mind if I don't get up for breakfast until lunchtime?'

'Do exactly as you like. It's your home for as long as you need it. I hope, for your sake, it won't be overlong.'

Pondering this somewhat ambiguous, maternal statement, Jane went upstairs to her room.

CHAPTER FIFTEEN

SHE awoke the following morning at eight o'clock, however, feeling fully rested and alert. She mused that it was ever the way; one's bed was only truly desirable when one knew one must leave its cosy softness and go to work. At such times it took a cold shower to rouse one fully to wakefulness.

Jane felt extremely tender towards Elaine this morning and wanted to go and hug her immediately. She knew, however, that her mother would not welcome sentimental outbursts at eight o'clock in the morning and so resisted the impulse, took a leisurely bath, had an even more leisurely breakfast and decided to catch the ten-fifteen to London.

She left word for Elaine that she would be back in time for dinner at home, when Harry was to be a guest, and dressed with care so that she looked svelte for her trip.

In Northingham one didn't bother to dress up quite so much; the accent was on comfort and suitability and one always had to be prepared for a Scotch mist sneaking over the border like the clansmen of olden time.

When she arrived in the metropolis she rang the hospital where Olga worked without more ado. After some delay Dr Wyatt was brought to the 'phone.

'Jane, darling, are you on leave?'

'Only for the weekend. I wondered if you could come out to lunch with me? You name the place and I'll be there.'

'Well—er—' Olga sounded the least bit unhappy. 'Actually I have a luncheon appointment, Jane.'

'Oh, then that's all right. I didn't give you any warning.'

'Well, it isn't that, and I'm really dying to have a gossip with you, but it's the very first time you-know-who has asked me. I'm like a kid who has been promised a trip to the circus. Had it been anyone else I'd have asked you along, but—'

'That's all right, Olga. I quite understand. I hope you have a wonderful time.'

'How about tomorrow?'

'I'm staying with Elaine. I don't think I shall go out tomorrow.'

'Monday—?' Olga sounded worried.

'No. I'm travelling back on Monday. It's not important, Olga. There'll be other weekends and you can tell me all about it then.'

'Yes, of course. 'Bye, Jane. Take care of yourself.'

Jane reflected, somewhat regretfully, that it was no longer important whether she and Olga met or not. They were each going their separate ways involved in their respective careers and making new friends. She doubted if they would ever meet again, unless it was by accident.

She went by Underground to the West End, determined to do some shopping before the stores closed. It was pleasant simply to window shop down Oxford Street but she was surprised how the city seemed to overwhelm one after an absence. She had fogotten how to cross the road at the right time and was twice hooted back on the pavement by indignant motorists.

Turning into Regent Street she spent some time looking into the windows of Garrads, the jewellers. If her mother insisted on marrying Harry it was no use giving them a conventional gift. They each had a house and chattels of their own, so a personal gift to each would be more appropriate.

How about a pair of those exquisite onyx cuff-links for Harry and a bracelet for Elaine, who loved jewellery of all kinds.

'I had better save up like mad,' she said to herself, and was then aware of the tall reflection behind her own in the shop window. She turned with a stifled exclamation.

'This simply has to be the hand of fate,' Richard Graves told her seriously. 'I know one is supposed to meet everyone one ever knew if one stands in Trafalgar Square long enough, but I have only been in this shop for five minutes and yet I find *you* outside, of all people.'

Unaccountably Jane's hand was in his being squeezed hard.

'I didn't know *you* were coming south, sir.'

'I do come quite often; conferences and dull medical luncheons, things like that. I travel north overnight.'

'Have you a dull medical luncheon on today?' Her voice broke with laughter. She felt suddenly very happy.

'No.' He hesitated only a moment. 'Have *you* any plans?'

'None,' she dimpled, 'and nobody to find me something else to do, having made them.'

'Then,' he offered her his arm, 'we mustn't look *this* gift horse in the mouth. Where shall we go? The Ivy? The Cock? Even the Ritz?'

She chuckled.

'Anywhere at all. Where would you have gone if you hadn't met me?'

'To my club. But having met you I shall take you somewhere more in keeping with your elegance and charm.' She gave a little bow in acknowledgement. 'If you will excuse me a moment I'll telephone a Head Waiter or two. We don't want there to be no room at our particular inn.'

He soon rejoined her, hailed a taxi and handed her

inside with a sigh of obvious satisfaction.

'We're going to the Willow Room,' he told her. 'I always take attractive young women to attractive places.'

'Have there been many such trips, then?' she teased him.

'Surprisingly few,' he answered her seriously. 'Perhaps a couple during my medical school days. Then I lost the magic—until now.'

He reached and squeezed her hand in silence. She didn't question anything. If magic had been lacking in both their lives it was certainly present now. They had come together apparently by accident and they had created an aura outside of which nothing seemed either important or demanding.

The Willow Room was new to Jane, though she had heard of it. It was so lacking in ostentation as to pass almost unnoticed, unless one were looking for it. But the somewhat uninspired façade hid an interior which was an admixture of British discretion and good taste. The motif of the willow pattern was only hinted at in the decor, apart from the light shades which diffused a blue and yellow light upon the tables. The menu included the best of Chinese, French and English food, which accounted for the cosmopolitan clientèle of the place.

'It *is* attractive,' Jane agreed as she sipped a Martini. 'I must remember this place.'

'No,' Richard told her sharply. 'Don't come here again unless it's with me.'

This she queried, naturally.

'I have a somewhat unreasonable yet painful desire to have you remember me, Jane.'

She toyed with the stem of her glass. There was no Lyn to distract this moment away from her.

'I shall always remember you, Richard,' she assured him. 'Whether I come here again or not.'

The waiter came for their order and Richard almost mouthed a 'damn!'

'Jane,' he said, when the man had gone. 'I must admit that I don't really understand women. Their ups and downs, their come hithers and go thithers in the same breath, so to speak, confuse me utterly. If you had met one of your old acquaintances today in the same circumstances, would it have meant as much to you as this?'

Her heart was doing its best to prevent her speaking, but she had to reply even though she choked on the words.

'I would rather be here with you than anyone, Richard.'

For a moment, as he heard and understood her words, his eyes lit with little flames and he had to close them to put these out before they consumed his reason.

He fumbled across the table and she reached out her own hand and put it, like a fledgling into the warmth and security of the nest, into his.

'I love you, Jane. I can't explain it. It just happened. I think on that first evening when we worked at the accident, together. I decided if it was going to happen to me, it would be you who could do it.'

'I love you, too, Richard. I've been waiting for it to pass, feeling miserable, but it hasn't got any better.'

'Perhaps it's chronic,' he smiled tremulously. 'And termination is death.'

Their hands slid back to deal with slippery table napkins as the waiter arrived with the prawn cocktails they had ordered.

They picked about happily but hunger had passed with the truths now exchanged between them.

They both spoke at once.

'Jane, why were you so casual about—?'

'Richard, why were you so cold, when—?'

They laughed, their questions unfinished.

'Let's start our "Once upon a time" from today,' he suggested. 'And please may we have our "Happy ever after" as soon as possible?'

She flushed and lowered her eyes.

'All this,' he said in wonderment, 'and I haven't even kissed you properly yet. Jane'—he tugged her to her feet as the surprised waiter hovered—'an urgent engagement,' he explained, together with a few banknotes. 'My fiancée and I have to go.'

'You're mad,' she chuckled, as he hustled her along the pavement, relishing that proprietorial 'my fiancée' and also thinking it must have been an extremely benign fate which had also blessed Olga with a previous and preferred luncheon engagement. 'Where are we going now, Richard?'

'To find a park. We've been talking far too long as it is. I want to get away from people.'

But any London park on a Saturday afternoon is the Mecca of the garden starved city dwellers, and in Green Park there were literally thousands of parents and children feeding the ducks, despite the warning notices. The benches were crammed with the middle aged, the elderly and the just tired. There was less room here than on the streets where—now that shops and offices were closed for the weekend—there was suddenly a surprising calm, particularly on the pavements.

The lovers walked, scarcely noticing where they trod, and it was in the gardens of the Temple, in cool quietude, that Richard finally drew his love into his arms and laid his lips hungrily upon hers.

'I want to marry you now, today,' he told her as they finally drew apart. 'Have you any objections?'

'None, personally, darling. I think Northingham might have.'

'Oh, Northingham.' It was another dimension, a million rather than three hundred miles away at that moment. He kissed her again before he really thought about it. 'I suppose there have to be snags. What are yours in particular, pretty Jane? Is your mama extremely possessive of her treasure?'

Jane actually laughed out aloud.

'On the contrary my mama has just told me to mind my own business while she plans her own marriage to Harry. I think I told you about him.'

'Courageous mama. Still, in sickness and in health, I believe they say?'

'We'll say it one day.'

'And mean it, no doubt, at the time. It's easy to promise something when you feel sure it'll never happen.'

'That's cynical, Richard. I couldn't stop loving you because you were ill.'

'Or I you. But we're both in rousing health. There are other things which can happen to try a relationship, and other people, sometimes. I can quite believe my luck, Jane, and that's a fact. I have come down from cloud seven to cloud six. I feel vulnerable and not a little apprehensive. Perhaps I'm too old for you.'

'Rubbish! You're not anything of the kind. If you are wishing to break our non-existent engagement you'll have to think of a better one than that.'

'Sweet Jane, I don't! I'm afraid of you, and what you can do to me now, not of myself.'

'Then stop worrying this instant,' she commanded him, 'and kiss me again. Then we must talk and decide what is to be done about all this. I want to marry you, too, as soon as possible. But how soon *is* possible? It's

four o'clock already. Time is flying too fast and before
we know were we are you'll have to catch your train. Oh,
Richard, if only we could always be together!'

'They do say absence makes the heart grow fonder,
sweetheart.'

'Yes, but of whom?'

He lifted her chin and soon had her laughing again. It
was so easy to shed all problems and cares with the
beloved at one's side, and so easy to don them à
thousand-fold as his train steamed out of King's Cross
into the northern night.

Jane stared after the train long after it had disappeared into the darkness and only slowly realised that
she had promised to be home to dinner. Being with
Richard, so unexpectedly, she had shed the burden of
responsibility, which we all carry around with us, day-
long, and learn not to notice. Now she donned it again,
feeling its weight to be twice as heavy, and hailed a taxi
to take her to Waterloo as quickly as possible.

CHAPTER SIXTEEN

It was midnight when Jane reached home and she was surprised to find Elaine and Harry in the sitting room drinking brandy and ginger together.

'So you've decided to return to sleep,' Elaine said coldly. 'You really needn't have bothered.'

It would have been so easy to get angry and huffy with one's emotions already raw and exposed like so many jumping nerves.

'I'm sorry, Mother,' she nodded in Harry's direction, 'but I met someone quite unexpectedly. I did mean to be back earlier.'

'You haven't been near a telephone all day, then?'

'I've been in town. I simply didn't think of it until it was too late. How are you, Harry?'

'You doctors always ask that, Jane. It's up to you to tell *us*. I'm fine—sometimes.'

'Harry's health needn't concern you at this hour if it didn't worry you earlier,' Elaine snapped, now openly hostile.

'I've said I'm sorry—' Jane felt she must either explode or confess what was really afoot. But to mention it seemed suddenly dangerous, as though a public acknowledgement of being in love made it less true in fact. 'Please forgive me, both of you,' she pleaded, and made her escape before there should be a scene.

She was actually trembling when she reached her bedroom. Elaine had, last evening, drawn close enough to her to explain any attachment. But Jane was still a little too reserved to draw as near to her mother and

confide her most private affairs. They had never been
like that together and it was something which couldn't be
learnt in a day.

Yet misunderstanding was equally intolerable. She
wanted the world to know that she, Jane Pilgrim, was at
last so much in love that she would never be the same
person again, no matter what the future held for them,
the lovers.

She heard Harry leave and his car drive away and she
was concerned for him, wondering how long he would be
able to drive without becoming a danger both to himself
and to the others, as had happened to Mr Hetherington.
Yet, she told herself, aware that Elaine was mounting
the stairs and wondering if she would call in to continue
their quarrel, it was not as though multiple sclerosis was
a sentence of death. It was more a slow languishing, its
progress perhaps indiscernible from month to month.
Most victims grew quite old before they died of a
perfectly normal senile complaint. It was silly to fret
about people as though their problems were one's own
personal concern. Harry had Elaine; perhaps a new
and more sincere Elaine in that her second marriage
would be an affair where she had to be the strong and
dominant partner; and no doubt there was a Mrs
Hetherington behind the patient Richard had made her
concern.

She was able to settle her mind with these thoughts
and also realised that her mother had gone straight to
bed. In the morning they would talk and everything
would seem better for having been slept on. Meanwhile
there was everything to remember about this most
wonderful of days. Sleep would have been an unwel-
come intruder to rob her of such a mental banquet, late
though the hour might be.

They had decided, she and Richard, to keep their

attachment quiet for the time being.

'I have certain people to inform in my own way and time,' he had told her, and she had immediately thought of Lyn Forrester and wondered what really had been between them, and if it had been even remotely as wonderful as this? With Richard's hand firmly around her own her ponderings had brought her no qualms; now, however, she felt an uncomfortable thrill of jealousy, almost of insecurity. Lyn couldn't have made it all up about herself and Richard, surely? If not, what had gone wrong? Jane knew that Lyn spread her favours around most generously, so it could be that Richard was looking elsewhere for consolation when she had come along.

She hid from this thought wishing, now, that she had decided on sleep rather than heart searchings which merely made her feel miserable.

It was almost as though she didn't believe Richard's declaration, nor her own responses. It had all been too sudden to assimilate and everything would be wonderful again when she and Richard were together and he was telling her he loved her once more without urgency or the need for separation.

Dawn was breaking before she actually slept, and she awoke with blue shadows below her eyes, wanting to rush north with all speed and hurl herself into Richard's arms, seeking assurance that what had been between them was the truth and not merely a mood born of a moment.

She felt more sensible after her bath, however, and got up to make breakfast as the daily help did not come in on Sundays.

As soon as she heard a faint stirring in Elaine's room she was upstairs with a tray laid daintily yet bearing the most frugal of fare, for her parent did not eat much for breakfast. There was a pot of excellent coffee, however, and fingers of well buttered toast.

'Good morning, darling,' Jane greeted, stooping to kiss the other, who looked at her sharply after almost turning away from the salute. 'It's a lovely day. Is Harry coming to lunch? I'll be cook.'

'Harry'—Elaine said coldly—'is probably never coming again. Yesterday he was of the same mind as you about our marriage; that it would be a disastrous association from my point of view if he should become an invalid. You almost might have kept your threat to tell him his future,' she added bitterly.

'Oh, Mother, I didn't speak to Harry about anything,' Jane said quickly, feeling disturbed. 'I had come to understand your feelings in the matter and appreciate the position. Loving somebody very much is really all that is important.'

'You have suffered a change of mind, then?'

'Every woman's prerogative.'

'It would have been better had you at least been present to inform Harry of it. He has gained the impression that you don't exactly approve of him.'

'I think we should ask Harry to lunch, insist on his coming,' Jane said firmly. 'As to my not approving of Harry, that's neither here nor there. If *you* approve it's none of my business.'

'How magnanimous children are becoming!' Elaine's parthian shaft followed Jane down the stairs, and she sighed as she dialled Harry's number and waited for a reply to the ringing tone.

Harry's manservant answered first, then Harry's heavy breathing sounded in Jane's ear.

'Will you come to lunch, Harry? About one.'

'Thank ye, Janie, but I was only at your place last evening. You'll have plenty to talk about with your mother. She doesn't see ye often.'

Harry's half-squire, half fox-hunting type voice had always irritated Jane. She controlled her irritation now and persisted.

'I was really very rude last evening, Harry, not turning up to dinner. I do apologise most humbly. Please come, for *my* sake. I really want to chat with you about my mother. I'm worried about her and you.'

'Don't worry, me dear. I see your point and it's all off. I—'

'Harry! Don't be a fool. That's not what I meant. You and Elaine need each other like strawberries and cream. She's unhappy and utterly impossible, today. Unless you come round I—I'm going back north immediately, as soon as I can get a train,' she blustered.

'Janie, me dear, don't get so excited,' he said, obviously mollified. 'I would do anything for your darling mama, and she knows it.'

'She would also do anything for you, Harry. Remember that. One o'clock, then?'

After telling Elaine that Harry was coming to lunch in two hours' time, she donned an apron and surveyed the contents of the fridge. There wasn't time for a roast but the chicken pieces would be ideal cooked *à la Maryland* with banana fritters and onion and apple rings. There was melon to start with and she would make a fresh fruit salad for the sweet.

Jane excelled at all dishes cooked on the surface of the oven. Having lived so long in 'digs', dependent on a gas ring, she had learned all methods of frying and how to obtain the best results with the greatest variety.

Elaine made an appearance on one occasion and half-heartedly attempted to interfere. Jane dismissed her sharply, however.

'Do your nails, or something, Mother. I'm quite

happy on my own and we'll only spoil something between us. Perhaps you would lay the table when it's
time.'

As Jane washed up after the lunch had been declared
most successful and delicious, leaving the two middle
aged sweethearts sipping liqueurs with their coffee and
looking coyly at one another, with both secrets and
promises in their eyes, she held a conversation with her
dead father, waiting for his replies to her questions and
almost convinced that she actually heard them. She had
done this ever since his death, in times of stress, and
Elaine, once catching her at it, had decided that she
obviously wasn't quite right in the head.

'Dad,' Jane began quite seriously, polishing the glasses
with a special cloth. 'You know how you warned me that
one day I would have to tackle the Hill of Difficulty, as
we all must? Well—I always thought that would be my
job, but I'm not finding that so difficult at all. I'm taking
it in my stride. It's only part of my difficulty; because I
feel I must carry on with it, taking my MD and so on, as
you did; and loving Richard, maybe getting married
fairly soon, may prove awkward. You see, Dad, I know
Richard will be satisfied with no less than *all* of me, and if
I'm his wife, maybe having babies, how can I be true to
my career? It may get shoved aside, and I can't bear to
think of that. Neither can I bear the thought of losing
Richard or even quarrelling with him about anything. So
what must I do?'

'Supposing you talk all this over with Richard?' she
then imagined the answer came to her pleas. 'He's the
one vitally concerned.'

'Of course, Dad!' she exclaimed happily. 'I must
always talk things over with Richard from now on. I
somehow can't realise that this wonderful thing has
happened to me. It was like something dropping out of

the sky. Now I must go and have a heart to heart with Harry. You don't really mind about Harry, do you?'

She didn't even wait for the answer to this, knowing fully well that her father had not been a dog-in-the-manger type. He would always bless anyone who contributed towards his loved ones' happiness.

The conversation with Harry, while Elaine wrote letters, was much easier than Jane had expected. His health problems had sobered him up considerably and he had brought his legally trained mind to bear on his future with analytical precision.

'I may eventually become helpless, Jane, but I will never be a vegetable. I know myself, you see, and I shall always maintain a fight. You think I'm a bit of an ass, I know, but most of that has been a show. Lawyers are dull as ditchwater, really, and I thought Elaine liked my clowning. But it isn't really *me*, and now I believe Elaine was only encouraging me out of kindness. We both know and like each other. A lot better for all that has happened to bring us down to earth. Perhaps we really could make a go of it if we're not expecting life to be a continuous ride on the Big Dipper, all screams of excitement.'

'I'm sure you could, Harry,' Jane said softly. 'Mother loves you very much. I know that, now. Life is so much like a tossed salad, isn't it? You never know what will come to the top. But having the necessary equipment, in your case loving enough, I'm sure everything will be fine. I hope so.'

'I never expected to receive your blessing, Janie. I was always scared of you. You were eternally disapproving.'

'I know,' she said ruefully. 'A repressed schoolmarm attitude. I was a real little prig. You don't need my blessing, Harry, but you certainly have it for what it's worth, now. I suppose I've grown up a bit lately.'

'You should do it more often,' he smiled at her, teasingly. 'It becomes you.'

CHAPTER SEVENTEEN

'You know, this is a rum business,' said the man in the First Class compartment, opposite Jane. 'This typhoid scare. Now it has turned up in the north-east.'

'Really?' asked Jane. She hadn't got around to reading the weekend papers. 'Where is it?'

'About six suspected cases and one confirmed case, in County Durham. It travels, doesn't it?'

'No,' Jane felt bound to demur. 'It can only travel via an infected person or a carrier. This may be an entirely separate outbreak. Until the authorities have found the source of infection one can't really speculate.'

'There's been a lot of it about this year. At one time we never heard of it. It was under control, like smallpox.'

'It is more or less under control now.'

'How do you mean?'

'Well, enteric fever, as *we* call it, is more easily brought under control by modern drugs. At one time it was a killer. It's still bad, of course, but not fatal in the majority of cases. You can have a preventive injection, of course, if you're worried.'

'I'm going through to Edinburgh, so I don't think I'll bother, thank you, Doctor.'

The journey passed pleasantly enough and every mile brought her nearer to Richard. She counted the signal boxes and the rhythmic clatter of points, and then they rolled into the station at Newcastle, with which she was now quite familiar.

'Dinna miss yor connection, Doctor,' her porter

friend hustled her along to where the Northingham train was waiting. Soon bits of Hadrian's Wall could be seen lying atop the green, rolling hills to the north.

What pleasant country it was in late spring, with everything blooming two weeks later than in the south. If one travelled back and forth, Jane pondered, one could enjoy two springs and two blossomings. It was almost worth the journeying to experience such bounty.

Though she hoped Richard would meet her she dared not believe that he would. He was a busy doctor, not only concerned with serving two hospitals and a Nursing Home but with a private practice, also. She supposed he must have a partner in this venture, but it was surprising how little she really did know of him.

She felt a thrill of excitement as the train drew into Northingham and then saw that there was no Richard on the platform. Well, he obviously couldn't be there to meet her or he would have been. Unless it was a little too obvious for them to meet and greet one another on a station platform.

He would be outside in the station yard with the car.

But he wasn't. Her heart sank a little as she realised Richard wasn't anywhere in the vicinity. She felt vaguely let down in spite of the allowances she had made for his not being there. Then an unfamiliar car drew out of the parking lot and slid to her side. She heard a voice which jarred with its note of familiarity.

'Hi, Jane. I thought I would come and meet you for old time's sake. Are you surprised to see me? I thought you would be.'

'Kent!' Jane exclaimed in utter disbelief. 'What are *you* doing here?'

As she slid into the passenger seat beside her ex-tutor she feared the worst and yet hated to hear it from his own lips. Before he explained his presence, however, he had stooped and kissed her purposefully, as though reminding her that their past relationship had been based on such demonstrations.

'Aren't you glad to see me,' he demanded. 'I detect a certain frigidity in your mien which didn't used to be there.'

'Of course I'm glad to see you, Kent,' she said quickly. 'I'm simply so surprised. No—don't keep doing that,' she forbade, as he loomed over her once again. 'I—I hate casual kisses.'

'Believe me, honey, they needn't be casual.' His eyes began to twinkle at her as she fidgeted. 'You're such a little puritan, Jane,' he told her, 'and I find you most attractive. Shall we go and have a cup of tea somewhere before I deliver you at the hospital?'

'Yes—yes, please, let's do that,' she urged, playing for time. She wanted to meet Richard, who must be expecting her at the hospital or have left some message for her, but she couldn't face him until she knew more about Kent's arrival on the scene. This was a distraction for which she hadn't allowed.

'Well,' Kent told her in the small café where they sat partaking of tea and cakes, 'I got a bit fed up with teaching. The Principal was equally fed up with yours truly after a few barneys we'd had, so I decided to go back to the practical side of things. Northingham rang a bell with me; I couldn't at the time think why; and then when I came for my interview I saw your name up on the "call" roster. When the penny had dropped I decided I would like a job here very much, so meet the new CO, Jane, newly arrived last Saturday and fully prepared to help brighten your serious young life up a bit.'

'So you're the new Casualty Officer?' she asked faintly. 'Congratulations!'

'You don't sound terribly enthusiastic, my dear.'

'I—I—you didn't actually come because of me, did you, Kent? I mean there was really nothing much between us and I never encouraged you to think . . .'

'You have a new boy friend,' he accused her. 'That's it, isn't it?'

'No—er—it isn't that at all,' she fibbed.

'Who can it be?' he pondered, wrinkling his brow. 'There's the dashing young lad who looks like a matador and has an awful Midlands accent; there's the one with the hair and the awfully affected one with the teeth. I can't quite see you with any of them, Jane.'

'Because I'm not,' she said sharply. 'I didn't come here to carry on with the housemen. I'm working for my MD, Kent, and I can't afford distractions. In any case I'm only here for another seven months, then goodness knows where I'll be. Your contract must be for at least three years.'

'That's right,' he smiled. 'I don't understand you, Jane. You're like a hedgehog, all rolled up against attack. Can't you relax with me? Ours may not have been a grand passion but I thought it promised well. Now you're slapping my face repeatedly. Have I grown horns, or something?'

'Of course not. I—I'm looking for more than sex, Kent, to be frank, and you can't provide it as far as I'm concerned.'

He smiled a little ruefully.

'My ego takes another dip. You're telling me, ever so nicely, to run away and play, aren't you, Jane?'

'You have always been a great help to me in my career, Kent, and I'm grateful. I simply don't want you to be misled.'

'Don't worry, dear. All hope is from this moment abandoned. I shall expect you to be exceedingly kind to me while my broken heart heals.'

'Hearts were never involved with us, and you know it,' she now smiled at him, feeling glad to have got the matter off her chest. 'I don't believe my being at the infirmary had anything to do with your decision, either. The money must have been better, or the perks.'

'The trouble with you, Jane,' he wagged his finger at her admonitorily, 'is that you have lost the romance in your soul. I'm glad I found you out in time.'

As they drove up to the hospital she felt almost affectionate towards Kent. He had taken things so well and was quite good-humoured about it all. He could be fun, too, and would, no doubt, brighten the common room considerably.

She thanked him for the lift and then hurried off seeking the tall, dark clad figure she hoped would be awaiting her. After fruitless searching, however, while trying to be unobtrusive about it, she heard from the head porter that Dr Graves had left the hospital about six.

'Just when I was wasting my time having tea with Kent,' Jane fumed.

There was no message for her in the letter rack, either. It was as though Richard didn't care about her return. He had simply done nothing whatsoever about it.

A moment later Jane almost bumped into Lyn Forrester.

'Well, hallo! Had a nice weekend?'

'Very nice, thank you,' Jane replied civilly.

'Your boy friend found you all right, then?'

'My boy friend?'

'Dr Hillary has given us all to understand that he isn't your brother, Dr Pilgrim.'

'Oh, forgive me. He is a *friend*, of course.' She couldn't understand why she should find it necessary to emphasise the relationship. Now she wondered what, exactly, Kent *had* told the common room about her. 'I was just going to my room,' she added dubiously.

'Then I won't keep you. There's just one thing in case I forget to tell you tomorrow. *I* shall be helping in clinic, not you.'

'Oh!' Jane felt unreasonably disappointed and deflated. She liked doing afternoon clinic with Richard.

'You've had some experience, now,' Lyn went on casually, 'and that's all that was necessary. You'll be more use on the wards.'

Once she was in her own room Jane felt suddenly like weeping. Saturday was already such an age away that she began to doubt that anything untoward had happened on that day. She must have imagined everything, for obviously Richard couldn't care less about her today. She wanted to 'phone him, hear his beloved voice reassuring her on all accounts, but pride held her in check. She unpacked her weekend case, took a bath and finally threw pride to the four winds and 'phoned Hadrian's Retreat from the public 'phone box in the Outpatients' Hall. Richard's voice answered, cool and impersonal.

'This is Jane,' she told him lamely.

'Oh! Hello, Jane.'

'I—I thought you might have met me.'

'I heard you were being met. You didn't expect a crowd, did you?'

After her disappointment, her need of love and affection, his tone struck her like a blow in the face.

'Kent Hillary was my tutor,' she told him. 'I didn't know he would turn up here.'

'Obviously not.'

'What do you mean, Richard? What has Kent been saying?'

She sounded nervous and hated herself for it.

'Look, Jane,' he said coolly, 'I can't talk now. I have a guest. I'll see you tomorrow, I expect.'

'Very well. Sorry to have intruded.'

She knew this sounded childish but didn't care. She was hurt and offended and angry. Now she wished she hadn't taken the initiative and telephoned. Olga would have said 'Hang him!' and left any man to declare himself in unmistakable terms. Jane had as good as said, 'I'm in love with you. Please wipe your feet on me,' and Richard had promptly done so.

With the bitter taste of humbled pride adding to her unhappiness, Jane eventually went to bed with her head throbbing. She must have things out again with Kent, find out exactly what relationship her colleagues understood her to enjoy with the newcomer.

And on the morrow when she *did* see Richard she would keep a cool head and a refrigerated heart. Let him be the one to blow hot and cold as he had accused her of doing.

CHAPTER EIGHTEEN

THE following morning she was instructed to visit Dr Waddell, the pathologist, for a TAB injection.

'Everybody else was done yesterday,' he told her jovially, 'so there'll be a lot of sore arms and short tempers today.'

'Is enteric spreading in the north-east, sir?'

'They've raked in about another dozen suspects, but so far there's only the one confirmed case. Let's hope it stays that way.'

'Amen!' Jane said sincerely.

Lyn was halfway through the round on the women's ward, and obviously in a sour mood.

'You took long enough,' she accused. 'Perhaps you called in for a chat with your boy friend on the way?'

'As a matter of fact I didn't,' Jane said equably, making allowances for the fact that Dr Forrester was probably feeling the effects of her injection by this time. 'I had to wait Dr Waddell's pleasure. He wasn't quite ready for me.'

'Well, *I* feel rotten. Perhaps you can carry on alone while I sit down in Sister's office?'

'Certainly.'

'Call me if there's anything requires my presence.'

'Very well, Doctor.'

She was surprised to find that since Thursday evening there were several new faces in the ward. As Wednesday was admission day this meant the newcomers were emergencies and must therefore be studied carefully.

The first of these whom Jane saw was a young girl of about thirteen. Youngsters always looked somewhat out of place in a women's ward, but it was one of the hospital rules that children ceased at twelve and would thereafter be treated as adults. Jane noticed the girl grimaced at her and then rolled her head and grimaced at the woman in the next bed.

'It's all right, dear, don't be nervous,' she said soothingly, even before she had glanced at the girl's notes. From these she learned that Janice was suffering from chorea, an affection of the nervous system whereby all movement was spasmodic and involuntary. This was a complaint prevalent among studious and highly-strung children and most of them usually recovered on a treatment of complete rest and light diet in four to six weeks. Janice's case was complicated, however, by the fact that she was epileptic. She would need watching.

'Well, Janice, we'll soon have you right,' Jane said confidently, smiling down at the writhing figure in the bed. 'I must talk to Sister and see if we can't find somebody to read to you for an hour or two a day. It would help to pass the time, wouldn't it?'

'Yes, please!' Janice managed to mouth with difficulty.

'I'll come and see you again,' Jane promised, and moved on to Mrs Schofield, whom she already knew.

'How's the diet going?' she asked.

Mrs Schofield had been admitted suffering from obesity. She had become incapable of movement and weighed nineteen and a half stone while only being five foot four inches tall. She had now lost two stone and was having exercises ordered by the physiotherapist preparatory to getting on her feet again.

'Not bad, Doctor. I 'ad a nice bit o' tongue for my breakfast. My 'usband would say I got enough of that already. A long way off being slim, though, aren't I?'

'You'll walk the next two stones off,' Jane decided. 'Keep it up.'

The next of the newcomers was lying white faced against the pillows, nervously plucking the sheets and gasping rather than breathing. Sister Godolphin explained that Miss Thewell had been brought in in a state of collapse and was under observation. Nothing organically could be found to account for the collapse.

'Breathe naturally, Miss Thewell,' Jane said automatically. 'There's nothing wrong with your lungs.'

The woman closed her mouth and obeyed.

While Jane read the notes she surreptitiously studied the woman. A fifty-eight-year-old spinster, she might at this moment have been a typical victim of nervous dyspepsia and nothing more. Yet she had been found in the street in a state of heart failure and admitted to hospital. Something had to account for *that*.

As Jane asked for screens and passed her stethoscope over the flat chest she felt the woman's tension as though she was on the rack instead of a hospital bed.

'Please relax, Miss Thewell,' she requested. 'I'm trying to listen to your heart and you've put a coat of mail over it.' She smiled to put the other at ease and continued to examine the chest back and front.

'That's a very nice lum-te-tum,' she said at length. 'Nothing to worry about there.'

'No, so they all say,' Miss Thewell contributed nervously.

'But we'll keep you in until we're satisfied that you're really all right,' Jane assured her. 'Try to relax and knit, or read, or something. There's no need to lie down all the time. You're not ill.'

'But I collapsed—'

'I know, people who faint collapse temporarily, but

they're usually all right again quite soon. Don't worry about yourself, it was probably something quite trivial which may never happen again. Possibly you are run down . . .'

'Yes, I am. I looked after my dear father until he died early this year, not that I'm complaining, of course, because I only wish I still had him with me. But—'

'Yes, I do understand.'

Jane could not afford to stand talking with a patient whose real problems were not medical at all. There was still the men's ward and the private wing to tour and the respective Sisters would be on tenterhooks until morning rounds were over.

'It's close today, Sister,' she said as she mopped her brow. 'It feels like thunder.'

'It is looking rather ominous, Doctor,' Sister Godolphin agreed as they reached the ward office. 'Would you like a cup of coffee?'

Lyn was sitting leaning with her head in her hands at the desk, so Jane decided to press on with the morning's work without respite, though she did think her colleague was putting it on a bit considering there were many other members of the staff suffering similarly.

Her tour of the Men's Ward passed without incident, and she was just having a word with Sister Frear when she was summoned to the telephone.

It was Sister Godolphin.

'Can you come at once, Doctor, please? Miss Thewell has had some sort of attack and is in shock. Dr Forrester has wandered off and doesn't answer.'

'I'll come at once,' Jane decided.

She was conscious, as she hurried to the Women's Ward, that the storm had broken all around and was echoing among the border hills. The rain, also, was sheeting down, dancing off the roofs of outbuildings and bouncing almost a yard from the concrete of the parking area.

'Early thunder, harvest wonder,' she quoted a jingle from her childhood as she reached the ward.

There were already screens round Miss Thewell's bed and Jane made her examination quickly. The pulse was merely flickering and blood-pressure low. She asked for an injection of coramine to stimulate the heart and warmth to be administered in every conceivable way and in fifteen minutes the woman was looking more like herself and rolled a nervous eye in Jane's direction.

'Has—has it gone?' she inquired.

'Has what gone, dear?'

'The—the thunder.'

'It seems to be passing over.' Jane suddenly stopped in her tracks. 'Are you frightened of thunderstorms, Miss Thewell?'

'Terrified. I always have been ever since our house was struck when I was a child. I can't help it and since father's gone there's no one to—to—'

'Wasn't it thundering the other day, when—?'

'Yes, it was, Doctor. I ran out of the house and was taken ill in the street. I—I'm feeling better now.'

'It is my opinion,' Jane told Sister as they turned away, 'that this woman needs psychological treatment rather than physical. She's quite literally frightening herself to death.'

'How do you account for that, Doctor?'

'She admits she's terrified of thunder because of this unfortunate childhood experience. This is the first time she hasn't had her father to reassure and comfort her and I believe she panicked herself into a state of collapse on the first occasion and almost did it again today. There's nothing organic to account for her trouble. But un-curbed fear, as you know, can kill an animal or a young child. Miss Thewell has gone back to being a child again about thunderstorms.'

'There may be something in what you say, Doctor, but it's all very odd. Oh! There's Dr Graves in the corridor. I wasn't expecting *him* this morning. I'll have to go, Doctor.'

'You go along, Sister,' Jane said, trying to keep her own heart under strict control, 'I'll go back and have a word with Miss Thewell.'

The woman now had colour in her cheeks and was beginning to sweat profusely.

'Oh, Doctor, I'm so hot!'

'That's better, then, isn't it?' Jane smiled, removing a hot bottle and switching off the electric heating pad. 'I came to tell you not to be so frightened of thunder while you're with us, Miss Thewell. There are plenty of light-ning conductors on the building. I know it's a deep rooted fear with you and that my word alone won't cure it. But I want you to know that we're going to do something about it, putting the right people in touch with you and so forth. Perhaps you would like to see the Almoner with a view to asking if she can help find someone to live with you now that your father's gone? I'm sure it must be very lonely for you. We all feel better when there's someone at hand with whom we can discuss our feelings.'

'You're very kind, Doctor.'

'Try and rest, now, Miss Thewell. Let us do all the worrying for you.'

As she reached the office door she saw Richard perched on the desk in conversation with Sister. She would have walked by but the firm: 'Dr Pilgrim, one moment, please . . .' she could not ignore.

She looked past him and out at the steaming land-scape, trying to avoid those steel grey eyes.

'Sister tells me you have an interesting theory regarding our Miss Thewell, Doctor. I saw her when she was admitted, of course, but she didn't mention the effect thunderstorms have on her.'

Swallowing noisily Jane said: 'Fear of ridicule might have been a factor on that occasion, sir. It was driven out of her by a recurrence of the same conditions today. Also I was a new face.'

'And a very sympathetic one,' Richard murmured, causing her to glance at him suddenly in surprise. 'I don't think I need to see the lady, Sister, unless she makes a habit of it. I think Dr Pilgrim may well have put her finger right on the trouble. Notify the Psychiatrist and the Almoner and sedate her if the weather looks bad. One thing about our climate, it might well be freezing tomorrow. Are rounds over, Doctor?'

'I have the Private Wing to do, sir.'

'I'll accompany you, if I may, I'm lunching at the hospital today.'

It might have been her first day at the hospital in his company, so little did she feel she knew him. And yet last Saturday she had been in his arms and—

She trembled suddenly.

It could be quite a long walk to the Private Wing if one arranged it so.

'How are you, Jane?'

The man was speaking, now, not the physician.

'I'm very well, thank you.'

'Am I in the dog house?'

'Don't you deserve to be?'

'Jane—no one has any right to think he can go and meet *my* girl. I was jealous.'

Her heart began to soar.

'What *is* that fellow to you?'

'He was one of my tutors.'

'Nothing more?'

She swallowed. 'Am I asking you what you did with your life before we met?'

'*Touché*. But if I mind so much about so little please keep me in complete ignorance of your past *affaires d'amour*.'

'They have been so few and far between I don't think they need trouble you.'

He stopped suddenly half way down the long, tiled corridor and seized her hand.

'I love you, Jane. Can I say I'm sorry for the misery I inflicted on myself in not rushing to see you yesterday?'

'I was miserable, too,' she admitted.

'Then come to dinner and tell me about it.'

'I'd love to.'

He half reached towards her, remembered where they both were and passed a trembling hand over his head.

'Were we going somewhere?' he asked vaguely, at length, and she was amazed to discover she could laugh again and feel joy welling up within her.

'Oh, life and love!' she exulted. 'How they are tripping along together with me at this very moment! Life and love and the most wonderful and interesting job anybody ever had. His job, my job, our job. We can never be lost for something to discuss together. There'll always be a Miss Thewell or a Mr Hetherington when we're bored with each other. How could I even be bored with my Richard!' she exclaimed at herself for this absurdity. 'He's the most wonderful and interesting man in the whole world and I'm going to have dinner with him this very evening. Now I don't mind about missing the clinic. Life's absolutely wonderful.'

CHAPTER NINETEEN

'COME on to the canteen and I'll buy you a cuppa,' Kent Hillary invited.

As it was her first opportunity of challenging him regarding the gossip circulating about them at the hospital, Jane accepted with a gleam in her eye. It did not make her feel any better when they passed a domestic worker who winked broadly at her companion.

'Kent,' she began, as they sipped tea and ate scones, 'what exactly did you tell everybody about you and me?'

'I can't remember, exactly. It was all very casual over a few beers at the "George" on my first evening here. I mentioned that I had a girl friend working on the medical firm, and they told me you were on short leave. Why?'

'Well, they have me practically married to you, the nurses, housemen, everybody. It has been most embarrassing all day.'

'Good heavens! They must have a most active grapevine here. I couldn't keep a wife at the moment, but I would simply love to go through all the preliminaries with you again.'

His eyes gazed meaningfully at her and he covered her free hand with his own.

She wriggled free.

'Kent! It's that sort of thing which starts these rumours. One has to be careful.'

'I'll be careful, with a bit of encouragement,' he said eagerly, a devil in his eyes. 'I'll meet you up on the moors about ten.'

'Kent! Can't you be serious for a moment? I'm really very angry about all this. I want you to quash these rumours.'

'Why should I? They're all I've got and I'm hanged if I started 'em. You're being a little too pi for words, Jane. First of all we're kissing in corners; and I may add that to my recollection it was a mutual effort; and then when I follow up you're mortally offended by the very idea. Hang it, Jane! It's a woman's prerogative to say no, but she can't ask a chap to rub his own nose in the dirt into the bargain.'

He drank his tea offendedly.

'I'm sorry, Kent,' she said sincerely. 'Perhaps I am being too sensitive about all this. Gossip is always rife in a hospital and I've a pretty good idea who's keeping this titbit alive. I suppose Lyn Forrester was at your drinking party?'

Kent's eyes immediately lit up.

'Now there's a girl!' he decided with enthusiasm. 'She's tough and terrific, for all her blue eyed doll appearance. There are a few snags, of course,' he said speculatively, 'such as two kids and a boy-friend who carries big guns and with whom she's just had the most terrific row. I believe she walked out on him and now he's consoling himself with another.'

Jane's heart had contracted painfully.

'She doesn't always tell the exact truth,' she heard herself saying.

'What woman does?' Kent demanded. 'They're past mistresses at telling half-truths and leaving a chap guessing. Do *you* always tell the exact truth?'

To her shame Jane hung her head and declined to answer.

'Well, thanks for the tea,' she said at length. 'I must get back to work.'

'And about this evening? How about a real drink to show there's no ill feeling?'

'I'm going out this evening, Kent,' she told him. 'A prior engagement. I assure you there's no ill feeling and we'll certainly have that drink another time, I hope.'

She found herself brooding as she went back to write her daily report, however. Lyn's gossip that she had had a row with her 'boy friend' who carried big guns tallied with Richard's trip to London and meeting with her, Jane. But he was not the sort who would play one woman off against another, she felt convinced.

She wished she could know exactly what Lyn had meant to him, if anything, without appearing impertinently inquisitive or mistrustful.

When she was with Richard she trusted him implicitly and it always took other people or many-tongued rumour to shake her faith, not in him, but in the fate which had so surprisingly brought them together.

She was paying her final visit to the Private Patients' Wing when Sister Weller told her: 'Dr Forrester is looking for you, I believe.'

'Oh.' Jane's reaction was to think, 'No, she mustn't keep me late *this* evening, of all times.'

Lyn had realised as the day wore on that she could not play on her injection troubles all the time. Other members of the staff were carrying on with fortitude despite sore arms and—occasionally—attacks of giddiness. Jane's arm had become stiff and sore quite quickly, so by late afternoon they were all in the same boat.

'I'm off duty in five minutes,' Jane told Sister, 'and I have an appointment this evening. But I'll no doubt run into Dr Forrester. It can't be an emergency or she would have had me bleeped.'

All the medical staff carried small, battery-powered receivers in their pockets whereby they were kept informed by signal when they were needed urgently. Jane's signal was six short 'bleeps', and after ascertaining that her receiver was working normally she decided not to deliberately put herself in her senior colleague's path.

Deep down she knew she was in the wrong. Sister had quite clearly told her Lyn Forrester required her attendance, but she was aware that if Lyn thought she could put anyone to inconvenience and mess up their private plans she would do so without a qualm.

Therefore she was glad she did not run into her senior, who was on late call that evening, and made her escape to her room without a backward glance.

She spent some time dressing simply yet with great attention to detail. She wanted to look nice for Richard. While she was in the bath she thought she heard the 'phone ring in her room, but when she was dressing there was no interruption so she concluded she had been mistaken.

She started almost guiltily as she left her room and was accosted by a voice from behind her.

'And who's all this in aid of?'

It was Phil Wade, the gynaecological houseman.

'What do you mean, Phil?' she asked innocently.

'I mean you look ravishing, Jane. There's also that "*je ne sais quoi*" in your eyes which is never there for me.' He put a hand on his heart significantly.

Jane was pleased and yet disturbed by the compliment.

'I must normally look extremely homely if I merit such comments when I merely dress up to go out,' she shrugged. 'But thanks for pandering to my ego.'

'No, I mean it, Jane. Ever since a certain someone joined our ranks you have positively bloomed.'

'No connection,' she said a little stiffly. 'That's all your imagination, laddie. Goodbye for now.'

She sailed away, leaving him staring after her thoughtfully. To his experienced (experienced ha! ha!) eyes Jane was a woman in love. This Hillary bird had claimed to have parted from her with unfinished business on their hands. The housemen were now confidently awaiting the conclusion of said business. They took a lively interest in one another's emotional lives for which there was so little time for indulgence, a houseman's life being composed of seventy per cent work, twenty per cent sleep and the rest made up of extra-curricula pastimes and pleasures.

'Still,' he concluded somewhat enviously, 'you can make a lot of headway in half an hour if you both know where you're going.'

'Dr Wade,' Lyn Forrester's voice was like ice in his ear as she came up behind him. 'What are you doing outside Dr Pilgrim's room?'

He looked to his left in positive amazement.

'Am I?' he inquired rather cheekily. 'Is that a crime? I thought it was the obvious side to be.'

'Is she in there?' Lyn looked ready to do battle and Phil was glad Jane had made her escape as the other knocked sharply on the closed door.

'As a matter of fact she isn't,' he said clearly. 'She has gone out looking like a million.'

'Just now?'

'She'll be clear of the hospital by now,' Phil said confidently, hoping to aid his colleague in making her escape. 'She looked all set for one night of love, or whatever pretty women do in their spare time.'

'Don't be vulgar,' Lyn snapped. 'I'm not concerned with how she looked. She was told to report to me and she skipped off. I even 'phoned her room and there was no reply.'

'Can't you manage without her, then, Doctor?' Phil inquired with his tongue in his cheek.

Lyn realised she was being 'had'. This young man was enjoying the fact that the mouse had—on this occasion—escaped a very angry cat.

'I'll see her in good time,' she said, a menace in every word. 'And I'll manage very well without her, thank you, Doctor.'

If Phil had known where Jane was bound he would have 'phoned her, warned her, but as things were he couldn't help. His own registrar wasn't so wonderful but at least he wasn't eternally trying to score off his house-man, as Lyn Forrester did constantly. Oundle had told them all a few home truths about Lyn; how she used her dazzle to blind and then simply wanted her escorts as conveniences.

'I was beginning to be her blinking chauffeur,' Colin had complained, and continued in a higher falsetto: '"Darling, take me to my hairdressing appointment. I'll see you in two hours for lunch." "Darling, thanks for the lift but I see some old friends over there. Do you mind awfully toddling off on your own?" Enough is enough!' Colin had exploded. 'That woman only saw me as a convenient transport system.'

'Then it's all over?' Reg McArdle had asked with interest. 'I wonder what she would see in me?'

'What could anybody see in a microbe like *you*?' Colin demanded scathingly. 'You never even look washed.'

Reg's dark complexion and the fact that he needed to shave three times a day were a sore point with him. He immediately attacked with a few personal remarks about Colin's red hair.

'Pax, my children,' Phil Wade had said to them ben-evolently. 'This woman is not a bone for young dogs to snarl over. She's way over our heads and never gives us a

single romantic thought. If we step out of our class what
can we expect? A rap over the kunckles, that's what.
She'd be amused to think that we were heading for a
fisticuffs over her. Amused, lads, not at all concerned for
our broken heads. So let's shake and forget it, shall
we?'

'Are you a pup-surgeon or the Chaplain General?'
Colin had growled.

'I'm a disinterested spectator in the game where you
are making a fool of yourself, my lad.'

All hackles gradually subsided and the young men
went their several ways to cool off.

In the ward office of Women's Medical Lyn Forrester sat
brooding on the way her quarry had escaped her.

She had merely wanted to impose her seniority and
her will on Jane to ask her to stay on duty for a couple of
hours while she—Lyn—slipped out for cocktails. Lyn
would not have told her this, of course, she would have
concocted some emergency at home. But the fact was
that Kent Hillary had asked her to join him in the
'George' at half past six, and she was drawn to Kent,
possibly because she assumed he was primarily Jane's
concern.

'Is it a party?' Lyn had inquired.

'Lord, no. You and I would be sufficient of a crowd,
don't you think?'

'I'll try to get away,' Lyn had promised, allowing his
eyes to hold hers in a meaningful gaze.

But Jane had proved elusive and now Jane had
escaped. And if—Lyn suddenly pondered—she wasn't
dressed up for Dr Hillary, who was she donning her fine
feathers for?

She was all alone in the office with the impedimenta of
her calling around her. Lyn began to plan and ponder on

the mischief she could do Dr Pilgrim if she really tried, and so far, she told herself with some satisfaction, she hadn't even started to try.

CHAPTER TWENTY

OVER her coffee cup Jane glanced at the man she loved more than she could ever imagine loving anybody. She even pondered on the delight of pouring his coffee, as his wife, noting that he liked it black with a floating of cream on top and two lumps of sugar.

There was so much she needed to learn about him, but that was part of marriage, the learning, the adjusting to one another so that eventually they became a centrifugal force of all that was best in both of them.

'You're dreaming again, Jane,' he told her softly, smilingly.

'I know, and I like it,' she confessed.

The dinner had been a little frustrating for both of them who wanted only to be together. Not only was Griselda home for half-term, but a 'dear old bore', as Richard afterwards described one of his old medical friends, had decided to 'drop in and hope', his wife being away visiting her sister.

Now, however, Griselda had disappeared to spend an hour with her record player and the 'dear old bore' had moved on to chat with any other old bores who would put up with him.

'What will you do with such people after we are married?' Richard now asked her.

'Be nice to them, I hope,' she confessed, 'while praying they don't do it too often. Are—are we getting married, then, Richard?'

'You doubted my honourable intentions?' he countered. 'I'm afraid I'm old fashioned in that respect. I fall in love and I think only of marriage. The Sunday newspapers would dub me a very dull fellow.'

'You're never dull, Richard. I'm glad to hear you're still in love with me. I thought you might have changed after being angry with me.'

'"That altereth when it alteration finds"?' he quoted. 'Never. I was angry with myself that I could be so jealous. That Hillary's a personable young man and I suppose the trouble is he made me feel old.'

'Richard!' she chided him. 'You're always talking about your age as though you're ninety. Your age makes you what I love. Kent hasn't your maturity, and he never will have. He has a medical student mentality still.'

'Were you very fond of him once?'

'No,' she said rather shortly. 'I wasn't fond of him at all, really. A certain animal magnetism once drew us together for a short time. It was soon over.'

'Apparently *he* doesn't consider it's over. He lives in hope.'

'I've told him he needn't.' She looked across at him frankly. 'Richard, don't let us keep on talking about Kent unless you also allow me to question you about Lyn.'

'By all means let's have a confessional. What about Lyn?'

'Have you quarrelled with her recently?'

'I may have. Lyn enjoys a quarrel as other women enjoy chocolates. She is an expert at thrust and parry.'

'Are you in love with her?'

'While I confess to being in love with you? My dear, you must be joking. My heart is not so ambidextrous.'

'She's very fond of *you*.'

'I'm glad to hear it. I'm fond of her.'

'What am I to make of that?'

He smiled teasingly, chucking her under the chin.

'Whatever you care to, my sweet.'

'Oh, Richard. You're so maddening. I can be jealous, too, you know.'

'Of Lyn?' He looked astounded for a moment, then decided to play along with her. 'Then that's tit for tat,' he told her. 'We're both victims of the green-eyed monster.'

She looked at him so appealingly that he relented and found himself on his knees kissing her hands and cradling his dark head in her lap.

'You're all I want of all women, Jane,' he assured her. 'I can't even begin to think of how we're going to get round all the difficulties, but I know we can, and must. Just so long as I can see you occasionally and—' he drew her head down, dwelt for a long time on her lips, then sighed and put her hand, cool and small, against his cheek. 'Yes, the difficulties,' he pondered. 'I—I suppose you want to work?'

'Well, yes—for a year or two. I had thought you might offer me a partnership, when I'm qualified.' She chuckled.

'The sort of partnership I had envisaged doesn't require that MD you're after,' he said darkly. 'However, I do get your point. If you're going to work it had better be with me. Well, that's one hurdle over,' he said blithely. 'Now there's Griselda. How do you think you can cope with a sixteen-year-old?'

'I don't know,' she admitted. 'I don't think Griselda likes me very much.'

They were neither of them to know that Lyn had seen to it that the girl had good reason not to like Jane Pilgrim.

'There's time for you to get to know her better,' he decided. 'Some friends have offered to take her with them on a cruise, this summer, and she needs what she calls play clothes. Perhaps if you went shopping with her into Newcastle you might find she's not so bad.'

'That's an idea,' Jane said. 'Now what are the other snags to be discussed?'

'I can't think of any at the moment. So where were we before this conversation interrupted us? Oh'—he reached up and drew her on to the rug beside him relentlessly—'we were about to get to know one another a little better, I believe!'

Jane emerged from the embrace gasping and smoothing her hair, which was ruffled from masculine caresses.

'Richard! I heard the door close.'

He looked up, then drew her head down to his again.

'Darling, the door has been closed all along.'

'No. I mean that I heard it close. Somebody's seen us.'

'You're imagining things. Mrs Morrison would never barge in without knocking and Griselda's having a musical soirée, if that's what the din can be called.'

But Griselda was creeping back upstairs burning with the knowledge that her Uncle Richard was kissing that 'Pilgrim' woman. Lyn had told her that Jane Pilgrim was 'after' her uncle, that she had all kinds of plans for Hadrian's Retreat and her, Griselda. When she had Uncle Richard completely under her thumb it would be dreadful for all concerned, Lyn included.

'I thought *you* were going to marry Uncle Richard,' Griselda had stated. 'You said you would see to it that I took a course for models in London. You promised.'

'Things haven't been the same since Jane Pilgrim came among us,' Lyn had replied. 'And I have my pride. I'm not forcing myself upon your uncle if he doesn't want me, and if I have no influence with him I can't see that you get your model course, can I?'

Which was why Griselda had been extremely cool towards Jane on this evening, answering her questions with monosyllables yet being extremely verbose with her other table companions.

'It would have been fun with Lyn,' she now decided, biting her nails and wondering how she could stop things developing between her uncle and Jane.

Eventually she shut herself in the dining room and spoke long and unhappily into the telephone.

''Phone!' said Richard, as he and Jane strolled in the scented dusk of the garden at about ten-thirty that same evening. 'I'd better get it. Everyone else is in bed.'

Jane gulped in breaths of night scented stock and thought dreamily about getting back to the hospital after this enchanted evening. Being so much in love was wonderful and—as Richard promised—there were no difficulties to their marriage which were insuperable, given time and patience.

'Jane,' Richard said from the french window, sounding serious. 'It's Lyn. Will you speak to her?'

'How did she know I was here?' Jane wondered. 'I didn't tell anyone.' She picked up the 'phone. 'Dr Pilgrim here.'

'Ah, yes. Dr Pilgrim. I wanted to see you *before* you went off duty.'

'Did you?'

'Sister Weller says she mentioned it.'

'I—er—I believe she did. I was off duty at six this evening.'

'A houseman is off duty, Dr Pilgrim, when he—or she—is told to go by someone in authority. In your case that authority was me.'

'I—I'm sorry, Dr Forrester. I'll remember in future.'

'You have more than that to remember. You left no

movements chitty with the porter. Are you ashamed of being at Hadrian's Retreat?'

'Not at all. Why should I be?'

'It's you who are being furtive, not I. If I'm having dinner with Richard I say so, quite openly.'

'Is that all?' Jane asked, trembling with anger.

'No, it isn't all. You admitted a Mrs Purcell today.'

'Yes, that's true.'

'Well, nobody can find her admission notes.'

'I filed them, as usual.'

'I'm telling you nobody can find them. They're not here. I'm still hanging about on the wards trying to get a coherent story out of a comatose woman. Perhaps you'll deign to come back and help us to hunt the thimble? Or are you so much more pleasurably occupied?'

Jane slammed down the receiver, hard.

Richard was by her side, sensing her outrage.

'Why didn't you go and see Lyn when she asked?' he wanted to know.

'Because I would never have got here if I had,' she answered rashly. 'Lyn Forrester can't bear other people going off duty.'

'Isn't that rather silly?' he asked her. 'You have this chip on your shoulder about Lyn. I assure you she's quite a good doctor and not nearly so black as you paint her.'

'You're the opposite sex,' Jane said sharply, 'and so see her in quite a different light. I filed Mrs Purcell's admission card and treatment list. This is just a trick to spoil my evening.'

But when she returned to the hospital and went along to the female ward the file wasn't anywhere to be found. This involved ringing up the woman's family doctor and asking him to reaffirm all he had already stated in an accompanying letter, which was also missing.

'Don't you think you have been somewhat careless, Dr Pilgrim?' Lyn asked in front of Night Sister.

'It looks as though I have,' Jane said in her defence. 'But I'm sure I filed the documents. I always do. Shall I make a new card out while I'm here?'

'You had better do that, I think. Give it to Sister to file this time. I'm sure it must be your injection, or something, but you're certainly not yourself today, Dr Pilgrim.'

Jane began to doubt her own efficiency next day when her signature was discovered on a treatment card against a quantity of drug which would have killed the patient had it been administered.

'Three minims,' Lyn Forrester expostulated, 'is somewhat different from eight! I shall have to report this, Dr Pilgrim. You're obviously not safe to have around if you can make mistakes like this.'

'I'm sure I didn't—' Jane said weakly.

'And I'm sure you did,' Lyn lashed her. 'You're up in the clouds half the time and resentful of authority. You can't bear my telling you anything. I'm supposed to be off duty this afternoon and tomorrow, but how can I leave you if you're going to be criminally careless in my absence?'

'I promise it won't happen again, Dr Forrester,' Jane said quickly before she could lose her temper. 'You can go off duty with every confidence.'

'Anyway, what were you doing at Hadrian's Retreat last evening?'

'I was there by invitation,' Jane replied, then wondered how Lyn knew, and—if she minded—if it could have been possible for her to engineer these damning incidents.

'Of course!' she suddenly decided as Lyn sailed away. 'I know darned well that I would never put eight when I meant three minims. She overstepped herself a bit there. A three can easily be changed to eight. And the case-history was easy to "lose". They're not kept under lock and key like the drugs. I must watch out. It looks as though Dr Forrester disapproves of my visits to Richard and will stop at nothing to disgrace me.'

CHAPTER TWENTY-ONE

THE Senior Medical Officer of Northingham Infirmary, Dr Wattkin, had been absent on sick-leave almost the whole of the time Jane had been there. He had been back on duty for about two weeks, but was so deaf that he was not much use on the wards and was due for retirement in the very near future. He liked to read all case histories, however, and comment on them, especially if he didn't agree with treatments prescribed by the consultant.

When Jane was summoned into his presence next morning she was amazed to find that Lyn had actually written to him, setting down her complaints against her junior in no uncertain terms.

This left Jane at a considerable disadvantage for she knew how difficult it was to defend herself verbally against this written aggression. Like most deaf people Dr Wattkin did not care to admit just how little he could hear. He would, instead, fiddle with his deaf aid and accuse other people of mumbling.

From the outset Jane decided not to defend herself by accusing Lyn. She had no shred of proof and hadn't a hope that she would be believed. To make an attack on her registrar only two weeks before leaving the 'firm' might well prove to be disastrous; might well cause her to cut off her own nose to spite her face, for Mr France could decide he didn't want her with him on the surgical side if she had a reputation for carelessness, inefficiency and 'passing the buck'.

Therefore when Dr Wattkin asked her what she had to

say she leaned towards the 'loud-speaker' in his breast pocket and said clearly, 'Not much, sir. The three may have looked like an eight, but I'll be doubly careful in future and write very clearly with duplicated written figures in brackets.'

'Good idea!' he agreed, being glad that this young woman spoke softly and clearly rather than shouting at him. 'You can't beat your bosses, you know,' he advised lugubriously, 'so you may as well join 'em.' He laughed at his own joke. 'Yes, better join 'em,' he repeated, and dismissed her.

Back on the wards Lyn was obviously dying to know what had happened, but Jane volunteered nothing and so Dr Forrester asked her point blank.

'I had to report you, you know. What happened?'

'Nothing much,' Jane said airily. 'I shall not only put a figure but write my dosages out fully in future, and when you're about I shall ask you to confirm things, naturally. I can't explain the mystery of the missing file, but I'll also take great care about that, too, to ensure it doesn't happen again.'

'Good!' exclaimed Dr Forrester, rather disconcerted by Jane's frank gaze. 'I'm off for the next thirty-six hours, as you know, so please do be careful and call on Dr Wattkin whenever you want advice.'

'I will, Doctor,' Jane promised.

Lyn went home without any particular plans for her off-duty and feeling somewhat neglected by mankind in general. She decided to 'phone Kent Hillary to ask if he would care to join her for dinner, either at her own home or a restaurant. Sometimes men preferred home comforts after hospital fare, but Lyn hated cooking. The children had gone with her mother on a trip to the seaside, and would be staying overnight with her sister in Newcastle, so it was an ideal opportunity of having a tête-à-tête with the most attractive man to have come her way for a long time. Kent was attractive primarily because he had an apparent predilection for Dr Pilgrim's company, and secondly because he appeared to be a kindred spirit, not like Richard, who was so high-minded he would prove to be impossible to live up to.

Lyn had now, in her own mind, decided that Richard was not for her in other than the guise of friend and helpmate. He had resisted the more obvious of her advances for so long that she had finally desisted from making these in order to maintain her pride. She had minded that Pilgrim woman dining at Richard's house without her knowledge, however. It looked as though something might be going on behind her back, and though she had circulated the information that she and Dr Graves had had a profound disagreement, without actually naming him, she didn't consider he was sufficiently free of her to start taking up with someone else.

When the girl had 'phoned her last evening with the information that Dr Pilgrim was at Hadrian's Retreat, and that something had cropped up which necessitated their meeting as soon as possible, Lyn had been livid. How dared Richard invite the Pilgrim woman when he hadn't invited her, Lyn, for ages? Also, what could the wretched girl want her for? Lyn had made a friend of Griselda for her own purposes; she knew that Richard was extremely fond of the girl and that the way to his heart was through his niece's approval. Therefore Lyn had made presents of make-up and trinkets and other things dear to a young girl's heart; had enthused about this 'pop' idol and that, had listened to the plans for being a 'model' and promised to influence Richard to this end and now the girl was requiring confirmation that she still had some influence with her uncle and to this end she was visiting Lyn during this afternoon.

Kent said he would be delighted to dine with Dr Forrester and would she join him for cocktails, first, at the 'Royal'. He was working until eight, he explained, but as they were both adults he was sure there was no hurry to conclude their evening's entertainment early.

Lyn felt encouraged and hoped she could get her hair set in time. It was a nuisance that Griselda had to come, but she would drag her along to the hairdresser's if necessary.

All the hairdressers were too busy, however, to accept casual appointments on that particular day, and so Lyn was glad when Griselda offered to set her hair for her.

'We all practise on one another at school,' she confided. 'And then if we look too glamorous we have to comb it all out again. Rather a waste of time, really. I don't suppose all this is for Uncle Richard's benefit?' she asked hopefully.

'No. I don't feel very friendly towards your Uncle Richard at the moment, Griselda.'

'Nor I,' the girl said soulfully. 'He's absolutely scathing about my career as a model, and yet you promised to fix it for me. He wants me to go on to university, of all things. I hate school. It's all so repressing. Lots of girls of my age get engaged and even married, instead of slogging away. You do know, of course, that he's in love with the Pilgrim?'

'He's *what*?' Lyn asked coldly.

'They were kissing and making love,' Griselda went on relentlessly. 'I opened the library door last evening and they never even noticed me. Why did you let her get him, Lyn? I don't think I'll ever forgive you.'

Though Lyn had nursed suspicions that more than friendship was developing between the two, having her suspicions confirmed was like a stab in the breast. She had decided Richard was not her type, but knowing that he preferred someone else, when he could have had her for the asking, made her want to howl in sheer chagrin.

How that wretched Pilgrim girl must be inwardly gloating, knowing she had Richard where she wanted him!

'So what can I do about it, Griselda?' she asked automatically. 'He doesn't have to ask my permission to kiss Dr Pilgrim. In fact I have found him rather a prig, lately, and gave him to understand that there's someone else for me.' She viewed the evening ahead as surety that her attraction for the opposite sex was not diminishing. Someone simply had to bolster her ego, after Griselda's revelation. 'Anyway, dear,' she added, beginning to lose interest in all but her own affairs, 'surely the remedy lies in your own hands? If you don't fancy Jane Pilgrim as a stepma, and *she* isn't the type to recommend a modelling career for a young girl, then leave home. *I* certainly would.'

'You know, Lyn, I can't get hold of my money until I'm twenty-one. What would I live on if I left home *and* school?'

'It need only be for a short while,' Lyn told her. 'I bet after a week you could come back on your own terms. Would fifty pounds help?'

'Oh, Lyn!' the girl's dark eyes glowed. 'How can I pay you back?'

'Don't,' Lyn said sharply, pressing the cash into the girl's hands. 'You must keep quiet about my part in all this. I simply want you to be happy and I'm sure your Uncle Richard does, too, at heart. If he thinks his precious Jane is going to be instrumental in driving you away he'll drop her like a hot cake.'

'Which will be cheap at the price,' Lyn decided when Griselda finally went away clutching the fifty pounds in her hand, not even daring to consign it to her handbag.

It had been decided that instead of returning to school on Tuesday, after the half-term holiday, Griselda would simply 'disappear' for a full week until she had won her point.

Lyn felt rather uneasy when she realised she had forgotten to ask the girl where she would be staying. She had been a very sheltered girl and really had no knowledge of the world outside of what she had read in magazines or gossiped of with her friends.

'Oh, she'll be all right,' Lyn decided hastily, not really prepared to worry about somebody who was no concern of hers from now on. 'Girls are all born sophisticated nowadays and can pretty well hold their own. Let *him* worry. I'm hanged if I'm going to.'

Jane glanced at the note Kent had sent her with mixed feelings.

'I've got to speak to you on a matter of *vital importance*,' he had written. 'Can you slip along to see me this morning?'

Whatever could Kent want her for? she wondered.

When it was time for her coffee break she went down to Casualty but only the junior was on duty.

'The boss may be either in the canteen or have gone to his room,' he said. 'He had a headache, or a hangover, I wouldn't know the difference.'

So it was that a few minutes later Jane was tapping on Kent's room door, which was on the top floor of the Resident's Wing. Women were not supposed to visit their male colleagues in their rooms, or vice versa, but such rules were only made to be broken, human nature being what it is.

'Are you there, Kent?' Jane called softly.

There was no reply, but it could be that Kent had taken aspirin and fallen asleep. It easily happened when one was constantly overworked and tired.

The room door was not quite closed so Jane pushed it open and stepped inside. But there was no sign of Kent. His bed was neatly made with his pyjama case lying on top of the plain green quilt. The fresh wind blowing on this June day was rattling the window, which was of the sash variety and opened some distance. Jane couldn't resist a peep down into the quadrangle where a couple of gardeners were busy. Her own view was quite different and—she thought—much nicer.

To her horror the draught she had created in leaving the door open wide suddenly slammed it shut with a loud report. She turned the handle but nothing happened. The lock had obviously jammed.

'Damn Kent and his note!' she said bad temperedly as she struggled with the door handle afresh. 'I've got to get out of here, but how?'

She went across to the window and shuddered away from the idea of making her escape that way. There was really nothing for it but to use Kent's house telephone and get herself extricated by more normal methods.

But what the hospital would make out of the episode she didn't dare to think.

CHAPTER TWENTY-TWO

KENT HILLARY came grinning down the aisle between the
beds in the Men's Medical Ward, and pounced on Jane
as she emerged from behind screens.

'I never laughed so much,' he told her. 'And the
trouble about a true story is that it's always so much
stranger than fiction. Nobody believes you, of course,
that you called in my room quite innocently. You had an
assignation with me and I locked you in pending the time
when I could wreak my will on you. That's the general
idea. It's sent my stock up no end with all the nurses.'

'Oh, Kent, I felt so awful while I was waiting for them
to take the door off its hinges. I simply didn't know what
to say.'

Kent laughed again.

'And what *did* you say?'

'That you wanted to see me and I couldn't find you.
That was the truth.'

'Oh, yes.' Maddeningly, Kent apparently found the
urgency not now so great. 'That'll do any time. But when
they told me a beautiful woman had been found locked
in my room it really made my day.'

Beyond him Jane saw Richard scowling his way into
the ward.

'You'd better go now,' she urged.

'Oh?' Kent nodded cheerily at the consultant. 'Good
afternoon, sir. Windy, isn't it?' He went off chuckling
and Jane's heart dipped into her shoes as she realised
that Richard would probably have heard of her
escapade.

'Is this Mr Blythe?' he asked distantly and disappeared behind the screens.

'What's the trouble?' as she joined him.

When they were back in the ward office and he was still cold and impersonal she said somewhat aggressively: 'There's no need to treat me like a criminal. I really couldn't help it, you know.'

He looked at her as though she was an idiot, she fancied.

'What on earth are you talking about?'

'I got myself locked in Kent Hillary's room. I was quite alone and it was an accident.'

He suddenly shook his head and passed a hand over his eyes.

'Not you on top of everything else, Jane,' he pleaded. 'I can't stick any more and keep on working.'

'What's the matter?' she asked in sudden concern. 'Aren't you well?'

'*I'm* all right,' he said impatiently. 'It's Griselda. She didn't go back to school. I saw her on to the train, as usual, and she simply didn't turn up at the other end where she was to be met. It's twenty-four hours, now, and I'm frantic. A sixteen-year-old girl turned loose can just about get into any kind of trouble. I simply daren't think about it.'

'Have you told the police?'

'Of course I have. They say leave it to them. What alternative have I got but to leave it to them? I simply don't know where to start looking.'

'Think, Richard, there must be a clue somewhere. Girls don't just disappear. Has she any other friends or relatives who would take her in? Have you made her angry? Teenagers take themselves so seriously and we're inclined to treat them as children.'

He gazed at her for a moment without comprehension, as though his wits were dulled.

'I've already contacted all relatives and friends that I know of,' he replied at length. 'As to making her angry, she has made me very angry lately with these ridiculous ideas of hers about being a model. I'm sick of that subject though somebody's obviously been encouraging her to think she has a hope. I don't expect she has mentioned it to you?'

'No. Unfortunately she didn't talk about it to me, or I would have pointed out that she's a bit young to be considered for a modelling course at sixteen. Perhaps you squashed her too hard, Richard.'

'Jane,' he appealed, 'please don't criticise. I can't stand it. I want her back. Please be constructive.'

'To run away she would need money,' Jane said promptly. 'Had she a bank account?'

'Her Post Office savings haven't been touched. As far as I'm aware she hasn't a penny. That's what is so frightening. She could have been taken away, I suppose, abducted.' He closed his eyes as though he couldn't bear his own thoughts.

'Possibilities are legion,' Jane said, putting her hand on his shoulder for an instant. 'But there's only one fact. She could hardly disappear from a train so it looks as though she has planned all this. You should really go home and wait for news, Richard. You're no good here.'

'What was that you said about being locked in somebody's room?'

'Oh, that was stupid of me. It's not important.'

She was thankful that he didn't appear to wish to pursue the subject and went off after telling her the treatment the new admission was to receive and leaving her in charge of it.

She 'phoned him during her tea break but there was still no news of Griselda. He didn't appear to wish to talk over the 'phone, and she realised she might well be keeping the police from getting through to him and so hung up after saying she would call round at Hadrian's Retreat when she was free.

The rest of the evening dragged terribly. There were no emergencies and the routine seemed endless before she finally reported to Dr Forrester and asked to be excused.

'I suppose you can go,' Lyn said grudgingly, and added more brightly, 'Which boy friend is it tonight, then, Dr Pilgrim?'

Jane coloured and then smiled, trying to match the other's tone.

'I never deal in numbers, Doctor. Too exhausting. Goodnight!'

So nobody was any the wiser as to how she was to spend her evening, she fondly thought.

'Both of you stew in your own juice,' Lyn murmured darkly as she watched her young colleague hasten off. 'I know you'll be holding his hand as quickly as you can get there, but if young Griselda plays her cards right you won't be doing it much longer, my lady.'

Richard appeared calmer when she saw him, but this was only a superficial control as she soon found out.

'Any news?' she asked.

'No,' he exploded. 'But they do say no news is good news, don't they? What I mean is they haven't found a body, or anything. That's something, I suppose.'

'I'm sure she's all right,' Jane said quietly, shocked, nevertheless.

'I hope your woman's intuition proves to be correct. I am the victim of masculine logic. A sixteen-year-old girl, a *pretty* girl, disappears into thin air, without any money, and there still isn't a clue after thirty-six hours as to her whereabouts. Perhaps somebody *is* looking after her, feeding her, giving her a good time. But it won't be for nothing. I dread what Griselda may be required to pay her unknown "benefactor". She's such a kid.'

In a thin voice Jane said, 'Girls aren't as innocent as they were a generation ago, you know, Richard. They learn about human biology and have sex instruction in school. Griselda wouldn't go off with a man at the merest beck. Even the little I know of her I would swear she has good sense.'

'If she does turn up I'll flay her alive,' he suddenly declared, his eyes flashing, 'and what a relief it'll be to do it. I've never laid a finger on that girl but this is a good time to start.'

'Let him think so,' Jane pondered, 'if it does him good. He would be so glad to see her he wouldn't even scold the little wretch.'

'Is Lyn working late?' he suddenly inquired.

'Yes. I believe she's on call until supper.'

'She hasn't asked once about Griselda. Everybody else is driving me mad with inquiries but Lyn appears to have written me and my troubles right off.'

'She's probably busy and finding out from the others what the news is,' Jane decided, still thinking her colleague was somewhat remiss in this respect.

Richard appeared calmer again by now, and looked at Jane as though he was seeing her for the first time.

'By the way, I heard you had to be rescued from Hillary's room this morning. Apparently you still seek one another out, even breaking hospital rules to do it.'

Jane felt firstly stunned and then exasperated. She had already explained the incident to him herself, and none of it had apparently penetrated at the time.

'Kent wanted to see me,' she said sharply. 'I don't even know what about.'

'Then don't let me keep you from finding out,' he said

promptly. 'By all means finish your business with Hillary to your mutual satisfaction and give us all a rest from these divertissements. I didn't think the situation in which you found yourself at all humorous, but the rest of the staff apparently did. Of course my sense of humour is somewhat out of proportion today.'

She knew that this attack was simply a relief from his own troubles, but it hurt her just the same. She wanted to offer him her love and the comfort of her presence, but not while he was metaphorically slapping her face.

'Very well, Richard, I'll leave you,' she told him, her underlip trembling emotionally. 'I'm sorry I can't be of any practical help.'

He watched her preparing to go, and though he longed to call her into his arms, tell her he was sorry through a torrent of kisses, his body felt too lethargic to make the physical effort of healing the breach he—not she—had caused between them.

It was as though, being already miserable, he wanted to torture himself to the limit so that there was nothing left whereby he could feel any worse.

She said goodnight softly and hoped he would have good news very soon.

He responded and groaned a little as he heard her car drive away. The long night yawned ahead like an abyss, and he had no recourse but to enter its darkness and endure whatever it might bring.

Jane was miserably sitting on her bed drinking black coffee when her room 'phone shrilled. She was glad of the distraction. An emergency at this hour would take her mind off things.

'Dr Pilgrim?' came the night operator's stilted tones. 'Can you come down to Outpatient's to take an outside call?'

'Certainly!' She was in her dressing gown, but this was a tailored affair and she obviously couldn't wait to dress. If Richard wanted to tell her he was sorry, or had some news for her, then there must be as little delay as possible.

The operator put her call through to one of the kiosks in the main Outpatients' Hall, which was quiet at this hour, though further along the main corridor there was quite a bustle in Casualty.

'Jane Pilgrim speaking,' she announced, and the operator's voice could be heard saying: 'Press Button A, caller, please.'

So it wasn't Richard. Jane felt curious as to who could be telephoning her at this hour.

A female voice inquired: 'Am I speaking to Dr Pilgrim, please?'

Her heart sank for some reason. It was obviously a relative of one of her patients ringing up to ask about mother or dad.

'Dr Pilgrim here,' she repeated.

'This is Griselda. Griselda Rayne.'

'What?' Jane almost dropped the receiver. Her legs felt weak all of a sudden and her stomach apparently turned over. 'Where are you? What have you been doing? Your uncle's frantic.'

'Is he?' Griselda sounded somewhat uncertain of herself for a moment, then she went on breathlessly: 'Dr Pilgrim, I ran away because of you and Uncle. I saw you in the den that night and I was shocked. I'm sure Uncle would have married Lyn if you hadn't come between them, and that's the way I wanted it to be.'

'I'm sorry you disapprove, Griselda,' Jane said quickly. 'We don't know one another very well, you and I, and I'm not trying to rush into your lives like an express train. I can wait. The important thing is for you to come home immediately. Where are you?'

'I'm not talking unless you promise me something.'

'Griselda!'

'No, listen to me! This is the second time that I've cut school and I'm for trouble in a big way when and if I come back. I'm not facing all that for no gain. If you promise to leave my uncle alone, to let everything be as it was, then I'll come back and take my punishment.'

'Griselda, you can't force your will on other people like this, make them unhappy. Come back and let us talk things over like sane beings.'

'No!' the girl snapped. 'I needn't come back at all if I don't want. I've made myself look much older and I can get work if I want to. In fact I rather like being on my own,' she added defiantly, then climbed down a bit to add: 'But I'm quite willing to call it all off if I have your word of honour to finish with my uncle.'

'How can we arrange your return, then, Griselda? I would like to tell your uncle you're all right immediately. He's in a terrible state about you.'

'Do you think he loves me better than he does you? I mean if he has to choose . . . ?'

'There's no need to force a choice, Griselda. Your place is with him. I retire and give you my word of honour to tell him so. Now, where are you?'

'There's a Police Station just opposite this call box. I'm going to give myself up, now. They'll tell Uncle where I am, won't they? I'll bet he's mad. Goodbye, then, and—and thank you.'

'Goodnight, Griselda, and good luck!'

As Jane backed out of the kiosk she realised that she had just quietly surrendered her life's happiness to hasten the pretty little prodigal's return home to the fold.

CHAPTER TWENTY-THREE

IT was a few days after this that Jane came face to face with Richard in the Staff corridor. Dr Rothwell, a consultant from Newcastle, had been attending to all the usual business while Dr Graves settled his domestic affairs. His erring niece had once more been accepted at her select school to take her 'O' level examinations like everyone else of her year. Had it not been for that, her headmistress averred, she would not have taken Griselda back again at any price.

The haunted look had left Richard's eyes but he looked grey and his eyes were hard and bright as though he had slept little.

'I got your letter all right,' he told Jane with a slight nod. 'I quite understand that you're mixed up about many things. I keep forgetting how young you really are. Still,' he forced a smile, 'all the best.'

'Thank you, sir.'

They went on in opposite directions, and Jane thought: 'Getting locked in Kent's room was really very useful in its way. It made me look as though I was on a seesaw between two men. And now I've apparently finished with a bump at Kent's end. I really must arrange that drink with him to give strength to the idea. Thank goodness I go over to Mr France on Monday! I don't think I could stick bumping into Richard often as things stand.'

She took morning coffee in the junior common room and listened to the gossip without taking part in it.

'We've got enteric in Isolation,' Phil Wade

announced. 'It finally reached even here. How is it a bug can find Northingham when one's relations never can? It amazes me.'

Typhoid, Jane pondered. It seemed ages since she had discussed the possibilities of an epidemic in the north-east with a stranger on the train. Now the Public Health authorities of Northingham would be busy tracing contacts and carriers before the disease should fill the small Isolation Block and overflow into neighbouring towns and cities.

'—he was passing his gut in strings,' Colin Oundle was saying soberly. 'But that was before antibiotics, thank God!'

'Who's the new redhead on gynae?' asked Reg McArdle. 'She's a smasher. I've just been in the linen cupboard with her. The finest pair of eyes I've seen in a long time.'

Jane felt like screaming and made her escape. Young men she suddenly couldn't abide. Richard had spoiled her for their inconsequent chatter and he, whom she had been forced to relinquish, was all she had wanted of mankind.

The bleep in her pocket suddenly worked overtime and she was overtaken by other doctors all hurrying towards Casualty.

'A general alarm,' somebody said bleakly. 'That means they want us on an outside job of some sort. This sort of thing always happens when I'm behind on my own work to start with.'

They groused and protested, but there was never any lack of volunteers for accident work. Usually the Casualty Officer, who was the recipient of incoming information from the police, knew exactly who—or what—was wanted and sent the others about their own business.

'Accident at the junction of North and Roman roads,' he told the assembly, pointing to the place on a wall map. 'Collision between a Jaguar car and a petrol tanker—'

'God help the one underneath!' Colin Oundle exclaimed for all of them.

'Yes, well, the Jag is a bit squashed, naturally. There's a bloke in it and the police say a little doctor might get to him with luck. That means you, Jane. OK?'

'O very K,' she assured him. There were packed bags kept at the ready in Casualty. All she had to do was to pick one up and climb into the ambulance.

'They're draining the tanker,' Kent proceeded, 'so while there's petrol about there's the element of risk. I'll go with you, Jane. Thank you, gentlemen, please carry on.'

Jane was strangely glad to be occupied with something about which there was an element of risk. She felt transcended above human fear in her own personal unhappiness. She was scarcely aware of the ambulance's warning bell or the speed at which it travelled to the scene of the accident with the roads magically clearing before it.

'Hell!' was Kent's comment as they both saw the tanker rearing over the crushed car. 'It would take a midget to wriggle under there. I'm not risking your neck, Jane.'

'Oh, I don't know,' she said, from the ground where she was lying and peering. 'I think I can do something.' She jarred her elbow on a piece of metal, the Jaguar's number plate, and stared at it in awful fascination.

'What's up?' Kent asked sharply, as she gave a small strangled cry.

'That's Richard in there,' she told him, now mortally

stricken. 'That's Richard's new car. He wasn't happy about the steering.'

Before Kent could comment she was clawing her way under the tanker, and towards the twisted metal as though beset by a thousand devils.

'Watch the glass, Doctor,' a police inspector warned her, but Jane didn't hear. In the semi-darkness under the tanker where the fumes of petrol were so strong they made her cough and choke, she wriggled her way until she saw a hole in the side of the car where a door had once fitted. As the roof was almost to seat level in the centre there wasn't much room to manœuvre, but Jane couldn't have been kept from reaching the injured driver if she had been twice as tall and plump into the bargain. She could see Richard slumped over the steering column and wriggled into the rear of the car, then pancaked out and slid until she was alongside him.

'Fractured ribs,' she decided immediately, the doctor coming uppermost in a flash. 'That may mean internal bleeding. From the lungs . . . ?'

His mouth, as she lifted his head back, was clean, so that was all to the good although not a conclusion that pulmonary haemorrhage must be ruled out. His pulse, as she reached for his wrist, was regular but very weak. There was considerable bleeding from the right temporal area where there had been most impact, and the way his right arm lay, rag-like and distorted, showed that this was fractured.

She could not wriggle into any position which allowed her to use the ophthalmoscope in her pocket, but this was hardly the time for a full clinical examination. Practical measures were those now called for.

'Jane!' Kent shouted. 'Are you all right in there? How's our friend?'

'I'm all right, Kent,' she called back. 'And Richard's

alive. Get my bag to me, somehow, and put a vacolitre of blood in it. I can just about shove a needle into his left arm without fracturing my own spine.'

'Willco.' A few minutes later his voice came again. 'We're putting everything on a plank and pushing it in your direction. The tanker's nearly empty and rescue gear's on the way. Can you hold on?'

'I can.'

Jane often wondered afterwards how she managed to both drag the medical bag into the car and set up the transfusion which obviously kept Richard alive while they were awaiting rescue. Somehow she found a vein and upended the vacolitre and fastened it with straps of Elastoplast to the damaged roof. Then, as the pulse flickered and fluttered, she injected coramine and a little later, when Richard groaned, a quarter of morphia. She even managed to scribble this information on a little pink card and tie it to a button on his jacket.

At one point the tanker shuddered and settled fractionally and she murmured a little prayer in case they were going to die together. Not that she was afraid but she would have liked Richard to know that she was there with him at such a moment.

Later still she seemed to be suspended in a vacuum. Her body, which had shrieked out with pain and cramp, and which was pincushioned with slivers of glass she had picked up on her journey under the tanker, was suddenly without any feeling whatsoever. Only her finger on her patient's pulse kept her informed that he was holding his own, and in this knowledge she was supremely content.

It was not hours, really, though it seemed like it, before a giant mechanical hand seized the tanker and lifted it bodily off its crushed victim, thus letting in the light and causing Jane to cry out in sudden pain. The same robot hand tore the roof off the car and then willing hands bore Richard gently away and Kent lifted Jane up and dropped her quickly as she yelled.

'Kent! You're sticking prickles into me.'

He looked at her, then, and swallowed noisily as he saw the blood clots where glass had pierced her soft flesh. She was grubby and shocked, suddenly blubbering like a small, tired child.

'Come on, honey,' he invited her softly. 'You need a bit of attention yourself, you ruddy little heroine.'

Jane had never expected to be a patient in the hospital where she was employed, but after sundry pieces of glass had been removed from her person she was ordered to stay on complete rest for at least a week.

Staff were accommodated in a wing attached to the Night Nurses' Home, where there was a modicum of quiet even during the busyness of the day. The Sister in charge of this wing, an elderly old dear, promised her newest patient that she would keep her informed of Dr Graves' condition several times a day. He was in a side ward attached to the surgical wing, and first reports on him were reassuring. He had a fractured pelvis and fractures of the right radius and ulna, but he was constitutionally strong and everyone had high hopes of his eventual complete recovery.

'It was a miracle by all accounts how he lived through it,' Sister said grimly. 'His car has gone for scrap, so I believe.'

The next day, however, the picture was rather less optimistic.

'Well,' Sister said. 'You know what delayed shock can do. They're poorly for a day or two and then the upward climb begins. Doctor's strong and he'll pull through.'

The next day Dr Graves had a high temperature and was 'unsettled'.

'He's calling your name,' Sister said quietly. 'Would you like to sit in a chair and I'll get a porter to push you along to see him?'

When Jane was pushed back again, feeling weak and dejected despite having held Richard's good hand for half an hour and whispering in his ear that she was there and loved him desperately, she was told a visitor was waiting to see her.

She did not even feel curious as Sister helped her into bed and straightened her coverlet. She felt outside of all feeling and drained of emotion. Her very heart was struggling to beat back there in the side ward with the man she loved. If he died her life might go on but she would never really be alive again.

'May I show your visitor in, now, Doctor, or are you too tired?' Sister asked.

'I'm all right,' Jane said listlessly.

She felt herself tense as Griselda Rayne came into the room, her eyes red with much weeping.

Both of them loved Richard, and it was as though the love became a single thing that—like water—sought its own level and overcame all obstacles to this end.

Jane opened her arms and the distressed girl crept into their embrace, breaking down and bursting into incoherent grief that only a fellow sufferer could really comprehend.

CHAPTER TWENTY-FOUR

IT was a golden day early in September and up at Hadrian's Retreat Jane, aided by Griselda, was preparing a welcome home meal for Richard, who was being discharged from hospital that day after almost eleven weeks.

Mrs Morrison, the housekeeper, had gladly turned over her kitchen to the two happy young things and was as excited as they in the prospect of the Doctor's return.

'He may be rather niggly with me if he feels really better,' Griselda said somewhat grimly. 'When I told him about taking the money from Lyn to go away, and then holding my disappearance at your head like a pistol, he grew quiet and said in an ominous sort of voice, "We'll discuss all that when I get home," and I didn't like the sound of that one bit. Of course I told him I was sorry for what I did, and he looked at me and said I would be a darned sight sorrier if you didn't forgive me for it. But you have forgiven me, haven't you, Jane? I mean you're not just nice to me because you're so nice yourself? You do like me a—a little?'

'I like you a lot,' Jane confessed, making the younger girl sigh with happiness. 'You did a silly thing. I do silly things. We all do silly things at times.'

'Just like a French verb,' Griselda laughed, whisking up a froth of eggs for an omelette. 'And I don't really care about being a model now. I think I would like to be a doctor and now that I've got my 'O' level maths and physics and biology, there's a chance, isn't there?'

Jane nodded.

'When they told me how you'd crawled under that tanker to Uncle Richard, with glass splinters in you and goodness knows what else, and how you'd given him a transfusion and injections and kept him alive, well then I felt you were like Edith Cavell or Florence Nightingale, so very brave, and I knew you must truly love him, too. I was terribly ashamed, Jane. So ashamed of myself I wanted to die at one time.'

'All that is past,' Jane said gently. 'And as long as we learn from our mistakes that doesn't make them so bad.'

'Is that a car now?' Griselda asked, pricking her ears.

Jane's heart began to flutter in anticipation. Richard had been a terrible patient since he had started getting better and was the despair of both the nursing staff and the doctors, but this was Richard, the man, who was expected home. He was clear of the hospital and the irritations its discipline had imposed even on him.

Also, how did *she* stand with him?

During these trying weeks she had spent almost all her free time in the side ward with him, and some of her professional time as Mr France's junior. As Richard was cheerfully rude to surgeons as a point of personal honour, she didn't think he had taken her professional attentions very seriously either.

But on a personal note very little had been said, though she knew that he was aware all was as it had been with her. During the dark hours he had cried out for her and she had always let him know she was there. As the picture brightened she had tried to encourage him. If he didn't think she was a shining light among surgeons he at least considered her the nonpareil of womanhood.

In her heart of hearts she knew that he was waiting to see how complete his recovery was going to be before he spoke to her of their future together; for her own part she was as determined to spend her life caring for him no matter what his condition. In this she was now of the same mind as Elaine.

'It's him!' Griselda called joyously from the hall, albeit ungrammatically. 'He's walking very well.'

Jane kept back in the shadows while Richard greeted his niece and then his staff, who were obviously delighted to see him back and looking so well.

He had weaknesses, of course; Jane had them mentally listed, but they would all improve with time and perseverance.

'Is—?' He suddenly saw her, shy, and making her escape back into the kitchen with an excuse about something boiling over.

'I'll have a chat with you later, Griselda,' he said solemnly, though there was a slight twinkle in his eyes. 'And this time *don't open doors*.'

'No, Uncle.' She laughed. 'I won't.'

He strode purposefully towards the kitchen, well aware of the therapy of familiar surroundings on his tired body. He felt really fine at the moment and knowing who was the other side of that door made him feel even better.

'Jane!' he called, closing the door behind him and leaning against it. 'What are you doing here?'

'Cooking you a light meal,' she said promptly. 'We don't want you getting ulcers.'

'Are you here as my doctor, my cook or my future wife?'

He had approached close to her, now, and tossed away the stick they had given him at the hospital, spinning her round to face him without more ado.

'Proposals will have to wait,' he decided. 'At the moment I want to kiss you and hug you as you deserve, my darling girl.'

'Richard,' she said, a moment later. 'Turn the gas off,

will you? Whatever is burning is terribly distracting.'

'I agree with you,' he said, obliging. 'Nothing should ever distract one from kissing. By the way, my darling, France is quite resigned to you taking a month's leave in October.'

'I don't remember asking him—'

'*You* didn't,' Richard said promptly. '*I* did. I told him we'd be on our honeymoon, with or without his permission.'

'You're terrible,' Jane laughed happily. 'But it sounds wonderful.'

'Remind me,' he told her soberly, 'to thank you sometime for all you did to make our honeymoon and our lives possible, Jane. I shall never forget . . .'

She hushed his mouth with a sudden light kiss.

'Just love me, Richard,' she bade him, softly. 'That's all I ask.'

He thought as they merged once more that now that Apollyon lay defeated behind them both, he would dedicate his life to keeping his particular little pilgrim safe in their Palace Beautiful for ever.